Friendship Troubles

Brittany was the first one through the door. "Meg, where were you?" she cried breathlessly. She had a stricken look on her face.

Amy marched across the room after her. "No, that's not the question," she said, glaring down at Meg. "The question is, what did you say to Cricket?"

Meg groaned. "Oh no! Did Cricket tell you?" she said. "But it was all a mistake. I was just so upset. I'm going to apologize. I'm going to call her right now." She flung her comforter aside and leaped out of bed. But Amy stopped her.

"Don't bother," she said. "It won't do any good."

"That's right," Brittany added. She looked nervously at Amy and anxiously at Meg. "Cricket said she was canceling the meeting and that you would know why." She stopped as if she couldn't bear to go on. "She said . . ." she began again hesitantly.

"Oh, come on, Brittany," Amy interrupted. "Just say it. Cricket is quitting the club!"

Hello, Jenny!

Hello, Jenny!

Susan Meyers

little rainbow®
Troll

For Joanne Ryder,
who knows all about fixer-uppers
and *friendship*

Hello, Jenny!

Chapter

Meg Kelly was flying. Not in the air, but down a glistening white, snow-covered slope. Icy crystals sprayed from her skis, and her long blond hair streamed out behind her. And far ahead, speeding over the shiny white snow, was Jenny! Meg put on an extra burst of speed. She had to catch up. But just as she drew nearer, another skier raced past, cutting between her and Jenny. Then—

Meg sat up with a start.

Her heart was pounding, and for a moment she wasn't sure if she was asleep or awake. She looked out of her bedroom window, high at the top of her grand-parents' big old house in the redwoods, half-expecting to see snow. But it didn't snow in Redwood Grove, not even in December. She tested her toes, wiggling them beneath her comforter. They felt real enough, all ten of them. And the early morning sunlight streaming through the window seemed real enough, too.

From downstairs she could hear the whine of the coffee grinder as her grandfather ground beans for his morning cup of cappuccino. From her little brother Kevin's room next door she heard rustling noises, as if some small animal was waking up in its nest. And from down the hall came the sounds of a door closing, a toilet flushing, and her grandmother—or maybe it was her mother—clearing her throat.

Meg rubbed her eyes and the last bit of her dream melted away. She was awake, and the sounds she was hearing were the same sounds she'd been hearing every morning for the last three months. And in just ten days, Jenny—her best friend in all the world—would be hearing them, too!

Meg could scarcely believe it. In fact, she hadn't believed it—not absolutely positively—until she'd read the letter that had been waiting for her when she came home from school yesterday. She could see it now, a folded sheet of white paper lying on her desk by the window. Looking at it from her bed—the same four-poster bed her mother had slept in when she was a girl growing up in this house—she was suddenly struck by a wave of doubt. What if she was wrong? What if she hadn't read the words right? What if Jenny *wasn't* coming?

Her stomach knotted up at the thought. She threw

back the covers, leaped out of bed, and dashed across the room. Shivering slightly, she snatched the sheet of paper from the desk. She could feel Jenny's eyes, dark beneath her curly brown hair, watching her from the photograph tacked to the bulletin board above the desk. Her mouth, turned up at the corners, seemed to be laughing. But Meg didn't care. Though she could practically hear Jenny's voice saying, "Don't be silly, Meg. Of course I'm coming," she had to be sure. Taking a breath, she unfolded the paper, then slowly and carefully read the words that she'd taken in so quickly and excitedly the afternoon before.

It wasn't a letter really, not most of it anyway. The heading at the top said *Westside Travel, 1300 Bay Street, Los Angeles, CA.* Meg knew where that was— in the shopping center just a few blocks from Jenny's house, and from her house, or what had been her house until she'd moved to Redwood Grove. Beneath the heading was Jenny's full name—Jennifer Elizabeth Snyder—followed by a bunch of numbers and dates. It was a travel schedule, printed out by the travel agent and mailed to her by Jenny.

As Meg's eyes took in the numbers, her stomach unknotted and she let out her breath. It was all here in black and white. Jenny would arrive at the San Francisco airport, just an hour's drive from Redwood Grove, on Flight 117 at 10:55 A.M. on Monday, December 27.

Beneath the printed schedule—as if to make sure that Meg didn't start torturing herself by thinking it was all some kind of cruel or crazy joke—was a note in Jenny's familiar handwriting: *Thank you, thank you, thank you!* it read. *And Cricket, Amy, and Brittany, too. Can't wait to see you! XXXOOO Jenny.* Next to the note she'd drawn a heart with the words *Always Friends Club* inside.

Goose bumps popped out on Meg's arms at the sight of it. She checked the schedule again just to make sure. But the words hadn't changed. Jenny would be here in ten days, and it was all because of the Always Friends Club.

Meg Kelly and Cricket Connors—who'd taken Meg under her wing when Meg first moved to Redwood Grove—had started the club after they'd discovered that their mothers had been childhood best friends, and that *they'd* had a club called the Always Friends Club. The purpose of their club had been to carry out money-making projects and pool the earnings so that each member would have more money to spend than she ever could have earned on her own. The moment they found out about it, Meg and Cricket knew they had to start an Always Friends Club of their own.

They'd asked Amy Chan, an old friend of Cricket's, and Brittany Logan, who was new to Redwood Grove, to join. And the rest was history. In just three months, they'd earned enough to give them each more than $100. Brittany had bought a camera, Cricket had adopted a dog named Buster, and Amy had put her money in the bank to save for sports camp next summer.

When it was Meg's turn, she'd known exactly what to do. She sent the money straight to Los Angeles, and the result was the letter she held in her hand. A round-trip plane ticket for Jenny and the promise of a whole week together. It all seemed too good to be true. At least that's the way Jenny had described it when they talked on the phone after she'd bought the ticket.

"I'm so happy, Meg!" she'd said. "Nervous, too. About flying on the plane all by myself. And about meeting Cricket and the others. Do you think that they'll like me? Do they want me to come?"

Meg didn't have to think for even a second before answering "Yes!" Anyone would like Jenny. She was exciting and fun, and full of good ideas. She could draw terrific pictures, turn perfect cartwheels, and she was pretty without being stuck up about it. As for wanting her to come . . . well, from the way Cricket, Amy, and Brittany had been acting, anyone would have thought that Jenny was *their* best friend, not hers!

In fact, ever since they'd earned the money for Meg, Jenny seemed to have become their main topic of conversation. No one talked about doing new projects anymore because they were too busy planning for her visit. Cricket—who for some reason was more excited than any of them about Jenny coming—wanted to go to the airport carrying a big HELLO, JENNY! sign. Amy and Brittany wanted to have a "Welcome to Redwood Grove" party and a picnic at the beach beneath Golden Gate Bridge. They all wanted to take Jenny on the ferry to Angel Island and to ride the cable cars up and down the hills of San Francisco. They wanted to go to the zoo, and the planetarium, and Marine World, and have brunches and lunches and slumber parties. As far as Meg could tell, she and Jenny weren't going to have a single, solitary moment to themselves. That was the problem. And that's why she'd come up with her plan.

Frowning at the thought of it, she reached out to pick up a pocket-sized teddy bear leaning against the pencil holder on her desk. Jenny had given it to her as a going-away present when she left Los Angeles. It had brought her luck and given her courage when she was scared about going to a new school and making new friends. Now, when her biggest problem seemed to be too many friends, it seemed ready to listen.

"I know it's not fair," Meg said, as the bear watched her through shiny black eyes. "But I have to do something. I can't let them just—"

"Talking to yourself?"

Meg jumped. The teddy bear flew from her hands. "Grandma!" she exclaimed, turning to see her grandmother standing in the doorway. "Don't do that!"

"Sorry," her grandmother apologized. "I didn't

mean to startle you. I talk to myself sometimes, too."
She smiled. She was wearing the blue flannel bathrobe
with pictures of seagulls all over it that Meg loved to
snuggle against, and her short gray hair stood out in
wisps around her pleasantly wrinkled face. "I just
wanted to be sure you were up," she said, as Meg
scrambled under the desk to rescue the bear. "Though I
should have known you'd be too excited to oversleep
on the last day of school before Christmas vacation.
Do you want Grandpa to pack you a lunch?"

"No!" Meg exclaimed, a little too quickly. She
crawled out from under the desk and put the teddy bear
back on top of it. Her grandfather, who was into health
food, was famous for his tofu and bean sprout
sandwiches, and Meg was becoming famous for
refusing them. "I mean, I don't need one," she
explained, not wanting to hurt Grandma's feelings,
though she wasn't too fond of Grandpa's food, either.
"I'm eating in the cafeteria. They're having turkey
today," she said. "And after that there'll be a class
party with all kinds of good stuff. Our teacher, Mr.
Crockett, said he's going to dress up as Santa Claus
and bring Rice Krispies treats in the shape of
snowmen."

"Snowmen!" Meg's four-year-old brother, Kevin,
appeared in the doorway beside his grandmother. His
blond hair was tousled and the bottoms of his plaid
pajamas were slipping off, but his eyes were shining

brightly. Kevin was always looking for something to be excited about, and at this time of year he didn't have to look far. "I want a Krispies snowman, too!" he said. "Can you bring one home for me, Meg?"

"I'll try," Meg promised patiently. She'd been getting a lot of practice lately being patient with Kevin, playing with him on weekend mornings and in the evenings after dinner so that her mother could spend extra hours working on her computer in the study. Taking care of Kevin wasn't something she exactly liked—after all, how many games of Candy Land could anyone play—but it was all part of her plan. She had to help so that her mother would be able to finish the big project she was working on before Christmas. Otherwise . . . But she wasn't going to let herself think about that!

"I'll do the best I can, Kevin," she said now. "But remember, you'll have your own party at nursery school. You'll probably get all kinds of treats. And after Christmas, you'll get to make a real snowman, too."

Kevin's eyes grew even brighter at the thought, but Grandma frowned. "Now, Meg," she warned. "You know you shouldn't count on that. And you shouldn't, either, Kevin. It all depends on whether your mother can take time off from work. Right now it's only a maybe."

"Maybe, baby, wavy, gravy," chanted Kevin,

paying no attention to what his grandmother had said, just having fun making rhymes. "Come on." He grabbed her by the hand and pulled her toward the wide wooden staircase that led from the upstairs to the downstairs hall. "Make pancakes for breakfast. Make pancake snowmen!"

Grandma smiled. It was hard to resist Kevin. "All right," she agreed. "But you'll have to help me. You, too, Meg. In fact you'd better get dressed and hurry downstairs or you won't have time to say good-bye to your mother. She's been up for hours already, working in the study. She has to leave early this morning because—" She stopped herself. "Oh dear, maybe I wasn't supposed to say anything about that," she murmured.

"About what?" Meg's mind went immediately to her mother's job. She didn't remember her ever having to leave this early for work at the computer software company. Had something gone wrong with the project she'd been working on? Were the programmers behind schedule? Was there some kind of delay? Was her boss going to make her work the week *after* Christmas, too? Meg didn't think she could bear it if he did. "Grandma, what is it?" she asked anxiously. "What were you going to say?"

Her grandmother looked flustered. "Oh, it's nothing," she replied, shaking her head. "Just that . . . no." She stopped herself again. "I am *not* going to get myself into trouble over this. I'll just let her tell you herself."

And with that she and Kevin, who'd started singing a nonsense song about pancakes and snowmen, were gone.

Meg felt a sudden chill come over her. She realized she was still standing on the cold floor in her bare feet and that the warmth from the heater in the hall hadn't crept into her room yet. But that wasn't the problem. It was her grandmother's words. What had she meant about not getting into trouble? She didn't like the sound of it. Whatever she'd been about to say, it couldn't have been good.

She put Jenny's letter, which she was still holding in her hand, back on the desk and started for the door, ready to run down the stairs after Grandma and Kevin. But then, out of the corner of her eye, she caught a glimpse of Jenny's face smiling at her from the photograph on the bulletin board. She knew what she was thinking. "Meg, you're letting your imagination run away with you again. Get a grip on yourself. Everything's going to be fine."

The soothing rhythm of Jenny's words stopped Meg in her tracks. She was right. "Everything's going to be fine," Meg said out loud. Then she took a breath to calm herself. Instead of dashing downstairs, she stepped into her slippers, pulled on her robe, and headed for the bathroom at the end of the hall.

C h a p t e r

The bathroom was Meg's favorite room in her grandparents' house, where she and Kevin and her mother were staying until they could find a place of their own. It had a round stained-glass window with a graceful design of lilies and irises, a huge white porcelain bathtub that stood on legs shaped like lion's paws, and a toilet that you flushed by pulling on a long brass chain. Meg loved how pretty and old-fashioned the room was. On any other morning she would have taken time to watch how the light shining through the stained-glass window fell in pools of green and purple on the white-tiled floor. But today she hardly noticed.

She used the toilet, quickly washed her hands and face, then squeezed a wad of toothpaste onto her brush. It reminded her of the snow in her dream. She worked up a mouthful of foam, brushing up and down and back and forth, trying not to think of what her grandmother had been about to say. There was no point in guessing, after all, when she'd find out soon enough. Besides, she already knew that no matter how much she wanted her plan to work, no matter how many hours she spent playing Candy Land with Kevin, there were no guarantees. That was one thing her grandmother was right about. Kevin shouldn't count on building snowmen and neither should she. But, oh, how she wanted to!

It had all started when her mother came home from work a few weeks ago and announced that her friend Maxine owned a cabin in the mountains at Lake Tahoe, right next to a big ski resort. She and her husband had a son about Kevin's age, and she'd invited all of them—Meg's mother, Kevin, Meg, and Jenny, too—to stay with her family the week after Christmas.

"I'm sure it would be lots of fun," Mrs. Kelly had said when she told Meg about it. "They're a nice family and there's skiing and tobogganing, and an outdoor ice rink at the resort. But I had to tell her I wasn't sure we could go. I know I won't be able to take off that week unless I finish this big project. I'm willing to work extra hours and try, but then there's the problem of your friends." She'd looked at Meg, whose eyes had lit up at the idea of a snow trip. "I'm afraid Maxine can't invite everyone. She doesn't have room. It would have to be just you and Jenny."

Meg spit the foam out of her mouth now and hung up her brush as she remembered those words: *just you and Jenny*. Her mother had no idea how wonderful that sounded. She grabbed a comb and ran it through her hair, thinking of how quickly she'd assured her mother that the other girls wouldn't mind. Then she'd worked out a schedule for taking care of Kevin, her mother had started putting in extra hours, and now . . .

She laid down the comb, trying to stay calm. She was *not* going to start worrying. She glanced in the mirror and squirted some mousse on the cowlick in her bangs to keep it from looking too dopey. Then she headed—calmly—back down the hall to her room. She could hear Kevin downstairs in the kitchen still singing about snowmen, with his grandfather joining in on the chorus. She opened her closet to look for something to wear, but her eyes refused to focus on the clothes. All she could see was her and Jenny skiing down the slopes just as they'd done in her dream.

Not that either of them actually knew how to ski, at least not very well. If they did go to Lake Tahoe they'd have to stick to the beginner's slope and take some lessons. But tobogganing wouldn't be a problem, and neither would skating. They'd spent hours together at an indoor rink in Los Angeles, and outdoor skating sounded like even more fun. When they got tired of that, they could help Kevin and Maxine's son make snowmen and snow angels, have snowball fights, maybe even build an igloo. Then later, when they were cold and really tired, they could curl up in front of the fire.

Though Meg had never been to her mother's friend's cabin, she was sure it would have a fireplace, probably a big one with lots of crackling logs. They'd drink cups of hot cocoa, toast marshmallows, and talk and talk and talk. That's what she really missed. Though she and Jenny had tried to keep in touch by writing letters and postcards and using the telephone on weekends when the rates were low, there was no substitute for being together. When you were together you didn't have to work hard gathering your thoughts and writing them down, or worry about filling every moment with chatter just to get your money's worth on the phone. When you were together, you could sit around without saying anything for as long as you wanted. And when you did talk, you sometimes said things that were really important—things that you couldn't tell anyone but your very best friend. There'd be plenty of time for all that in a cabin in the mountains far away from Redwood Grove. Time for sharing secrets and for being silly, too—for giggling and gossiping and sharing private jokes. Meg and Jenny together again, just the two of them. That was the important part. Two girls together, not five.

Trying to ignore the guilty feeling that crept over her, she pulled a pair of black and white checked leggings from a hanger, then reached for a bright red oversized sweater—one of her favorites—to wear with them. But as her fingers touched the fuzzy red wool, she stopped herself. The sweater was by Kiki Johnson, the children's fashion designer who the girls in the Always Friends Club had modeled for last month. Brittany, whose mother was a fashion designer, had gotten them the job, and that was how they'd earned the money for Jenny's plane ticket. Remembering that now, Meg pushed the red sweater aside and grabbed her old white cable knit. It wasn't so pretty and it looked as if it could use a good cleaning, but at least it wouldn't remind her of what a traitor she was.

She turned to her chest of drawers and started rummaging around for some underwear, trying not to think of what Cricket, Amy, and Brittany would say when she told them—*if* she told them. Of course, there really wasn't any "if" about it. She had to tell. She and Jenny couldn't just disappear. The trouble was, the longer she put it off, the harder it was to—

"Meg!" Kevin suddenly burst into her room. His pajama bottoms were still sagging and he was out of breath from running up the stairs, but his eyes were shining with excitement. "We're going to cook the pancakes. Come and see me make a snowman. Grandma says I can use raisins for eyes."

He didn't wait for a reply, but dashed back down the stairs.

25

Meg couldn't help thinking—not for the first time—how easy it was to be four. Maybe I should just let Kevin tell them, she thought, as she pulled off her robe and pajamas. He'd look so cute they wouldn't be able to be angry or hurt, or whatever it was they were going to be.

Meg got dressed quickly, layering a red cotton turtleneck under the sweater, and hurried downstairs, tying her hair back in a ponytail as she went. She reached the last step just as her mother came out of the study.

Mrs. Kelly was wearing one of the suits she'd bought when she started her job at the computer company—a blue-and-pink check—and despite the thick folder full of papers she was carrying and the reading glasses perched on the tip of her nose, Meg was suddenly struck by how pretty she looked. Was it her new hairdo—shorter, swept back, and highlighted with gold—or her figure, which was slim and trim after three months of aerobics at the exercise studio where Amy's mother taught classes? Or was it something else? Grandma had said she'd been up working for hours, but she didn't look tired. In fact, she looked as bright-eyed and excited as Kevin.

"Ah, there you are," she said, seeing Meg. She took the glasses off her nose and dropped the file full of papers onto the table in the hall. "I'm really making progress on this," she announced. "I'm almost certain

I'll finish it on time. My boss is going to be pleased. Maybe he'll even give me a raise!"

"You mean . . ." A feeling of relief swept over Meg. So the project wasn't behind schedule. She didn't have to worry. "Then why do you have to leave early?" she asked. "Where are you going? Grandma said that—"

"Oh no. Did she tell you?" Mrs. Kelly's face clouded over. Meg recognized the look in her eyes. Her mother and her grandmother didn't always get along, and living in the same house had been a strain on both of them. "This is just what I was afraid would happen," Mrs. Kelly said. "I warned her not to say anything. I told her I didn't want you to get your hopes up."

"My hopes?" Meg echoed. What was she talking about? The only thing she had any hopes of right now was the snow trip, and if her mother's work was going well, then that couldn't be what she meant. Did it have something to do with Christmas? Was she going shopping for presents? But the stores wouldn't be open this early.

Mrs. Kelly looked at the puzzled expression on her daughter's face. "Then you really don't know?" she said. "Grandma didn't tell you?"

Meg shook her head.

Her mother shook hers, too, but with a sense of exasperation rather than confusion. "Well, she might as well have," she sighed. "I was going to keep it secret until I was sure, but now I guess I'd better tell you.

27

Tim called last night." She paused and the look of excitement returned to her eyes. "He may have found a house for us!"

Meg heard her words, but for a moment they didn't register. Tim? A house? Then all at once she remembered. Tim Eliot was the real estate agent who'd been taking her mother around to look at houses. They'd gone out together almost every weekend— before Mrs. Kelly had started putting in so much extra time at work, that is—armed with maps and printed lists of houses. Mrs. Kelly had usually come back discouraged because houses in Redwood Grove were expensive to buy. Since Meg's father had died several years ago, the Kellys didn't have a lot of money to spare.

Meg had almost stopped thinking about a house of their own. She figured they'd just go on living with Grandma and Grandpa forever, which would be hard on her mom but fine with her. She loved this house with its beautiful rooms and the secret attic hidden away at the top (where she and Cricket had found the scrapbook that told them about the original Always Friends Club). And she enjoyed being spoiled by her grandparents, even if Grandpa's cooking was sometimes hard to take.

"Well, aren't you even a little bit excited?" Mrs. Kelly asked. "I know you like living here, but wouldn't it be great to have a place of our own? We could get all our stuff out of storage. You could set up your dollhouse again. And remember what I said about getting a kitten? You'd like that, wouldn't you?"

Meg had the feeling she was being bribed. "Uh . . . yes," she said. "Of course. But where is this place? What's it look like? When can I see it?"

"Well, that's more like it," said her mother, smiling. "But as I said, don't get your hopes up. Actually, I shouldn't get mine up, either. I don't know much about this house yet, except that it's a fixer-upper. That means it needs work. But the price is right and Tim wants me to see it. He's taking me there this morning. I'm supposed to meet him at his office in a few minutes. Of course, nothing may come of it," she added quickly. "That's why I wasn't going to mention it until I knew more. Little did I know your grandmother would—"

"Now, Janet, don't blame me." Meg's grandmother came out of the kitchen with Kevin trailing behind her. The smell of freshly brewed coffee and pancakes wafted after them. "If it was supposed to be a secret, you should have told me," she declared.

"And what would you have said?" Meg's mother turned to face her mother. "That I was just being silly or a worrywart or something," she answered herself, without giving Grandma a chance to reply. "Honestly, Mother, I don't know why you can't just let me—"

"Now, Janet, don't get on your high horse about

this." Grandma drew herself up. Even in house slippers she was taller than Meg's mother, and her spine was as straight as an arrow from years of practicing yoga. She could actually stand on her head. Meg had seen her.

"*My* high horse!" Mrs. Kelly exclaimed.

Meg saw two spots of color appear on her mother's cheeks. She tried to think of something to say. She knew Grandma could be unfair sometimes, and she didn't like to see her treating her mother like a child. But before she could find the right words, Kevin piped up, "No fights, no fights!" and Grandpa came out of the kitchen, an apron around his waist and a spatula in his hand.

"What's all this?" he said, his eyes crinkling in a mischievous grin. "Did I hear someone mention high horses? That sounds like something I heard twenty years ago. Only then it was about wearing a strapless dress to the prom and wanting to stay out partying until dawn."

"Dad!" Mrs. Kelly objected. "You know I was home by midnight, and as for that dress, it wasn't strapless. It had two little—" She stopped. "Listen to me," she moaned. "A grown woman—mother of two—defending her behavior at the senior prom!"

Grandma chuckled, and even Meg couldn't help smiling. But Kevin turned to his grandfather and said earnestly, "They were having a fight. They're always having fights."

"No they're not." Meg came to her mother's defense, though even as she spoke she knew it was true. Her mother and her grandmother did have fights, and lately it had been happening more and more often. "At least not *always*," she added honestly.

"Hardly ever," Grandma corrected her. "Isn't that right, Janet?" She looked at her daughter with a sudden fondness, as if remembering her as she was on the night of that prom. "We just . . . well, we just have different ways of seeing things, that's all. Now come on." She took the spatula from Grandpa's hand and herded him back into the kitchen along with Kevin. "Your mother has to leave and we have to finish making these pancakes. How about a snowman with M&M eyes?"

Kevin whooped excitedly at the idea of chocolate in his pancakes and disappeared into the kitchen with his grandparents.

Mrs. Kelly watched them go, then let out a sigh. "Sorry, Meg," she said, shaking her head as she grabbed her coat from the old-fashioned mahogany coat rack in the hall. "I didn't mean to lose my temper. But sometimes Grandma makes me feel like I'm ten years old again."

Meg wanted to understand, but it was difficult. She liked both her mother *and* her grandmother so much. "I guess I just don't get it, Mom," she admitted. "I'm ten years old and Grandma doesn't make me feel like that. In fact, sometimes she makes me feel a lot older than ten."

"I'm afraid it's not quite the same," said Mrs. Kelly with a weary smile. "But don't worry. As soon as we find a place of our own, Grandma and I can go back to being friends. We really are, you know. In fact, she's one of my favorite people. It's just living in the same house that makes things so difficult—for her as well as for me."

"Well, then I hope this place you're going to look at is good," said Meg. "And that we can afford it and all. I don't really want to move, but . . ." She searched for something positive to say. "But I would like to get my dollhouse back. And a kitten." Better not let her mother forget about that! "And it would be good for Kevin, too," she added seriously. "Grandma and Grandpa spoil him."

Mrs. Kelly laughed. "Well, they may do a little spoiling of someone else, too," she said. "But thanks, Meg." She slipped on her coat, picked up her folder full of papers, and headed for the door. "I appreciate your support, though this will probably come to nothing, just like all the other houses I've looked at. Still, at least I'll have tried. I'll find out today, too, whether my boss will let me take off so we can go to the snow with Jenny. I still feel bad about the other girls. Were they terribly disappointed when you told them?"

Meg felt her stomach turn over. With all the talk about houses, she'd forgotten about the snow trip and about telling her friends. Now here it was, looming in front of her again, and she wouldn't be able to put it off much longer. "Uh . . . no," she said. "Not really. That is . . ." She wanted to go on, telling her mother everything, but what could she say? That Cricket, Amy, and Brittany weren't disappointed because she hadn't given them a chance to be? That was the truth, but she was sure it wasn't what her mother had in mind.

Fortunately, Mrs. Kelly was more concerned about the time than about Meg's answer. "Well that's good," she said, glancing at her watch again. "Now I really have to go. Tim"—her eyes lit up again as she said the name—"is going to be wondering what happened to me. Have a great day at school," she called over her shoulder as she ducked out the door. "And remember, Meg, you're lucky to have found such wonderful friends!"

Now why did she have to go and say that?

Meg heard Kevin chattering to his grandparents in the kitchen. She could smell the pancakes, too, now chocolate-flavored from the M&M's. But the aroma didn't make her feel hungry. She wasn't even sure that she'd want the turkey dinner at school. She peered at herself in the hall mirror, half-expecting to see that her nose had grown long, like Pinocchio's. Though, of course, she hadn't really told a lie. But it was getting harder and harder not to all the time.

She could imagine how it would be when she met Cricket this morning. They usually walked to school together, meeting halfway between their houses. Cricket was sure to be full of her usual high spirits, bright red hair gleaming, blue eyes shining excitedly.

Cricket was *always* excited about something. It was one of the things Meg liked best about her. She'd chatter on about Christmas and the class party, about her dog Buster—*and* about Jenny.

Meg would try to steer the conversation in another direction, but she knew it would be hard. Cricket could almost read minds. She had a kind of sixth sense about things, and ever since she'd found out that she and Meg were practically sisters, and that they'd each had a best friend named Jenny (Cricket's Jenny had moved to Alaska before Meg arrived in Redwood Grove), she'd been convinced they were on the same wavelength. It was kismet, she said.

Kismet was a big thing with Cricket. It meant destiny, or the idea that things happened because they were meant to happen. Meg didn't quite believe it herself, but she had to admit that sometimes she wished it were true. After all, if things happened just because they were meant to happen, then you didn't have much responsibility for them—or much guilt, either—did you?

She leaned closer to the mirror. Her head seemed to ache and her face looked sort of pale. Maybe it was the white sweater she was wearing reflecting light onto her face. Or maybe she was getting sick. She stuck out her tongue to see if it was coated, then ran her fingers over the sides of her neck beneath her ears. Were her glands a bit swollen? Was her throat a little sore? Would it be better if she just stayed home in bed instead of going to school today?

That would mean missing a lot of fun stuff, like the holiday pageant, and the class party, and seeing Mr. Crockett dressed up as Santa. But it would also mean *not* seeing much of Cricket and the others until after Christmas. She knew that Cricket's family was leaving tomorrow to spend the holidays with relatives in Fresno. And Amy had tons of relatives coming to her house. She'd been complaining all week about how she wouldn't have time to do anything except take care of her little cousins. As for Brittany, her family threw lots of parties at this time of year, so she was sure to be busy, too.

In fact, it would probably be December 27—the date of Jenny's arrival—before they could all get together again. Meg stared at herself in the mirror as a plan took shape in her head. Suppose they went to the airport, all four of them, came home, and had some sort of party. Then, when it was over and everyone had met Jenny, she could tell them the news about the snow trip. She could make it seem like a spur-of-the-moment thing. That wouldn't be such a big lie. Especially since she wouldn't know herself if the trip was on until her mother got home from work today.

Trying, once again, to ignore the guilty feeling that crept over her, she rubbed her eyes to make them look bloodshot, and slumped in what she hoped was a feverish way. It wouldn't be easy to get past Grandma's eagle eye, and she'd have to be careful about Grandpa, too. Otherwise he'd whip up one of those broccoli, wheat germ, and carrot juice shakes that he insisted were the perfect cold remedy. The thought of gulping down the gloppy grayish mixture that would emerge from the blender almost made her lose heart. Was it worth it? Maybe she should just—

Suddenly the telephone rang.

Meg jumped. The phone was sitting on the table right beneath the mirror, and its ring was so loud that her teeth seemed to vibrate. She made a dive for the receiver just as Grandma called out from the kitchen, "Meg, will you get that? If it's someone from our bird-watching group, tell them I'll call back later."

But it wasn't a bird watcher. It was Cricket.

"Oh, am I glad I got you!" she exclaimed, her voice leaping out of the receiver and into Meg's ear. "I was afraid you might have already left."

For a moment, Meg's voice deserted her. She was glad that Cricket couldn't see the expression that came over her face. She struggled to put the thoughts she'd been having out of her mind so that Cricket wouldn't be able to put her sixth sense to work and pick them up over the phone. "No . . . uh . . . I'm still here," she said, regaining her voice and pulling herself together. "Actually, I'm feeling sort of—"

But before she could start describing her

symptoms, Cricket interrupted with a sudden shout. "Buster, no! Stop that!"

Meg held the phone away from her ear. She heard Buster, Cricket's big, shaggy white dog, barking in the background, then a scuffling of feet, and the sound of a door slamming shut.

"Sorry," said Cricket breathlessly, as if she'd been chasing Buster around the house with the phone in her hand. "I had to lock Buster in the laundry room. He's all excited because he knows I'm going somewhere and he wants to go with me. But I can't take him to the orthodontist. That's why I'm calling. At least it's one of the reasons. I've got an appointment that my mother and I both forgot about. She didn't realize when she made it that it would be on the last day of school. We have to go all the way to San Francisco. Anyway, what I'm trying to say is I'm not going to be able to walk to school with you this morning."

"You're not?" Meg, still staring into the mirror, saw a look of relief come over her face.

"Well, you don't have to sound so happy about it," Cricket said.

"Oh . . . oh, I'm not," replied Meg. "I mean, that's awful, Cricket. You'll miss the turkey dinner and the party. But don't worry," she said, quickly reviewing her plans. If Cricket wasn't going to be in school and if she didn't have to walk with her this morning, then there was no reason why she shouldn't go. She could handle

39

Amy and Brittany, especially with all the stuff that would be going on in school today. She didn't have to worry about them reading her thoughts. It was Cricket who was the problem. "I'll tell Mr. Crockett why you couldn't make it," she promised, trying to keep the excitement out of her voice. "And I hope you have a good Christmas. I won't see you until after that, so—"

"After Christmas? Meg, wait. You didn't give me a chance to finish," Cricket protested. "I'm not going to miss the whole day. My mother promised she'd get me back after lunch, or at least in time for the class party."

"Oh. Well . . ." Meg didn't know what to say.

"Yes," Cricket went on, too excited to pick up on the note of dismay in Meg's voice. "So there will be plenty of time for me to tell you about the other reason I called. I've got an idea, Meg. A really terrific idea for a club project!"

Meg's hopes began to rise. A club project was exactly what they needed. It would give them something to think about, something to do, something to take their minds off Jenny.

"Cricket, that's great," she said. "I thought none of us would ever come up with another good idea. What is it? Tell me."

But Cricket, who loved suspense, wouldn't. "Can't," she said maddeningly. "Not now. I've got to go. I'm not dressed yet and my mother's throwing a fit. I'll tell you as soon as I get to school, I promise.

Everyone's going to love this. Especially you!" And with that, she was gone, leaving Meg with a dial tone buzzing in her ear.

"Was I right?" Grandma came out of the kitchen as Meg replaced the receiver. "Was it a bird watcher?"

"Uh . . . no," Meg answered, still feeling dazed. "It was Cricket. She can't walk to school with me today."

"Ah," Grandma said. "Well, don't worry. Your grandfather can drive you when he takes Kevin to nursery school. You'll have to walk home, of course, unless your mother gets off work early. But maybe you can do me a favor. Could you stop at the florist—the one next to the dry cleaners—and get me some holly? I've been meaning to make a wreath for the door."

She took some money out of her purse and gave it to Meg, then began talking about getting the Christmas decorations down from the attic. Normally, Meg would have been excited about decorating the house for Christmas, just as she would have been about eating the M&M-studded pancakes that Grandpa and Kevin presented to her when she took her place at the kitchen table. But now she hardly noticed.

What was Cricket up to? she wondered, as she ate her pancakes and listened to Kevin chatter on about Santa Claus and snowmen. What kind of idea could she possibly have? And why had she said that Meg especially would love it?

Meg was still trying to figure it out when she got

out of the car in front of Redwood Grove Elementary School, waved good-bye to her grandfather and Kevin, and hurried up the steps and into the building. They'd been late getting started because Grandpa couldn't find his car keys, so the tardy bell was already ringing as she dashed down the hall. She slipped into her seat in Mr. Crockett's classroom—Room 5A—just as the loud clanging stopped.

A few other late arrivers ducked through the door. Meg caught her breath. As the hum of talking and laughter died down, she looked around her, first up at the huge papier-mâché whale—made by last year's fifth-grade class—that was hanging from the ceiling above her head, and then at the tanks of iguanas, gerbils, and turtles that lined one side of the room. She was disappointed to see that Mr. Crockett was wearing just a Santa Claus hat, not a full Santa suit. But the reindeer antlers that someone—maybe Mr. Crockett himself—had attached to the bust of George Washington perched on the corner bookshelf more than made up for it.

Amy Chan, sitting in the row nearest the windows in front of Cricket's empty desk, caught Meg's eye and waved. Her shiny black hair was tied up in two ponytails wrapped with red ribbons and decorated with tiny gold Christmas tree balls. She was wearing a bright green sweater and pants, rather than her favorite sweats from the Redwood Grove Junior Soccer

League. Amy's changing, Meg thought. Maybe it was the modeling they'd done for Kiki Johnson. Or maybe it was Mark Sanchez, the cutest boy in class, who seemed to have decided that Amy was a very interesting girl.

Meg stole a glance across the classroom at Mark, who looked as cute as ever, then slipped off her jacket just as Brittany Logan, sitting at the desk beside hers, leaned over and whispered, "Where were you?" Brittany's tawny blond hair swept the shoulders of her fuzzy red sweater, identical to the one Meg had decided not to wear. It looked beautiful on her, as everything did, and Meg was glad she'd worn her white sweater. Though she knew she'd never be as beautiful as Brittany, there was no sense inviting comparisons.

"Did Cricket call you?" Brittany said, still speaking in a whisper. Her eyes, shaded by thick, dark lashes, were shining. "She phoned me and Amy. She's all excited. She has some kind of an idea for a—"

"Brittany," Mr. Crockett interrupted. "Just because it's the last day of school doesn't mean we're suspending the rules. We have to work in the morning if we want to party in the afternoon." He tried to sound stern, but the Santa Claus hat on his head spoiled the effect.

Even Brittany, who hated getting into trouble, couldn't help smiling as she murmured a quick apology and then opened her math book. As soon as Mr. Crockett turned to the chalkboard, she mouthed the word *lunchtime* to Meg.

Meg looked across the room at Amy who nodded and mouthed *lunchtime,* too.

And that was that. It turned out that Mr. Crockett meant what he said, so there was no time to talk about anything except school work until they were in the cafeteria picking up their trays loaded with turkey, mashed potatoes, and cranberry sauce. Meg was glad she hadn't stayed home. If she had, she would have been choking down one of her grandfather's carrot juice shakes instead of reaching for a slice of cake with bits of candy cane stuck in its fluffy white icing.

"What do you think Cricket's up to?" she said, as they headed for an empty table. She didn't expect Brittany and Amy to know any more about the project than she did, but she wanted to get the conversation headed in the right direction—that is, *not* in the direction of Jenny's visit.

To her surprise, Amy answered, "Well, all I know is that it has something to do with helping someone— at least that's what she said."

"Really?" Meg felt a sudden twinge of jealousy. She set her tray down at the end of a table decorated with green and red balloons and a paper Santa Claus. "Cricket didn't tell *me* that," she said.

She saw Amy and Brittany exchange a glance as

they sat down across from her. She had a feeling that Cricket might have told Brittany the same thing she'd told Amy. But Brittany, like Kevin, didn't like fights, not even little disputes among friends. "Well, she probably didn't have time," Meg said quickly, sticking a straw into her milk carton. "I know she was in a big hurry when she called me. I guess we'll just have to wait until she gets here to find out. I think it's great that she's thought up something, though. We've been getting sort of lazy."

"I agree," said Amy, not wasting any time before digging into her food. She swallowed a mouthful of turkey and cranberry sauce before going on. "I was going to try to think up something myself after vacation, even though it's not my turn. It's not Cricket's turn, either, come to think of it," she added. "It's really yours, Meg. You thought up our first project, remember? Cricket did the second, then me, then Brittany. So now it's your turn again."

"I guess you're right," agreed Meg, sliding over as a bunch of noisy fourth graders plopped themselves down at the end of the table. "Only I've been so busy thinking about—" She stopped herself just in time. Cricket's project had been working like a charm so far. No one had mentioned Jenny's visit, not even once. She wasn't going to be the one to spoil things. "I mean . . . I don't care if she takes my turn," she said quickly, hoping no one had noticed what she'd almost said.

"I'm glad she's come up with a project. I just wish she wasn't being so mysterious about it."

"Well, that's Cricket for you," said Amy matter-of-factly. "She can be pretty annoying sometimes."

"But she doesn't mean to be." Brittany came to Cricket's defense. "She just gets carried away. That's what makes her such fun. Why, the club wouldn't be anything without Cricket. *N'est pas?* I mean . . ." She blushed as she always did when she slipped into French. "I mean, isn't that right?"

"Yes, of course," Meg said, wondering whether Brittany had turkey dinners in France, where she used to live. "But the club wouldn't be the same without you, either," she added. "Or Amy."

"Or you!" said Amy as she stole a piece of candy cane from Meg's slice of cake. "But let's not get all mushy about it." Amy hated sentimental stuff. "Let's just hope Cricket gets here—and soon!"

Cricket didn't, though. In fact, it wasn't until late in the afternoon, when the class party was almost over and most of Mr. Crockett's Rice Krispies snowmen were gone, that she finally burst breathlessly into Room 5A. Amy, sitting with Meg and Brittany in a circle of chairs near the gerbil tank, jumped up and waved as Cricket thrust a note into Mr. Crockett's hands.

"Well, I'm surprised you came at all," he said, looking up at the clock. It was fifteen minutes before dismissal time. "But grab some food, what's left of it, and sit wherever you want. It's party time!"

Not bothering to stop at the snack table, Cricket made a beeline for the chairs by the gerbil tank. Just a moment before, Mark Sanchez and a couple of other boys had been sitting there, but they'd left to scout out what remained on the snack table. Meg had been sorry to see them go, but now she was glad. "What took you so long?" she said as Cricket collapsed into Mark's empty chair. "What did the orthodontist do to you?"

"Oh, that was nothing," Cricket replied, waving her hand dismissively. She was wearing a red vest patterned with gold shooting stars over an orange turtleneck and tights, and she'd tied a pink scarf around her head. On anyone else it would have been too much, but on Cricket it seemed exactly right. "The appointment with the orthodontist went fine. I don't have to get braces until next year. It was the traffic that held us up. There was an accident on the bridge, and it took two hours to get across! My mother didn't think it was worth coming in, but I had to. I won't see you again until tomorrow, and I wanted to—"

"Tomorrow?" Meg interrupted. "But aren't you going to Fresno tomorrow?"

"Yes," Cricket replied. "But we're not leaving until noon, so there'll be plenty of time for a meeting at my house in the morning. Then we can discuss all the plans for this project," she said excitedly. "We won't be doing it until the week after Christmas, but—"

An alarm bell went off in Meg's mind, but it was Brittany who broke in. "Wait a second, Cricket," she said. "Don't go so fast. You haven't even told us what this project is. And I don't see how we can do it the week after Christmas. That's when—"

"Jenny's coming!" Cricket finished for her. "That's exactly what my project is. We'll take all the ideas we've been talking about," she said, not seeming to notice the look that had come over Meg's face. "Then we'll choose the best ones and plan out Jenny's visit, down to the last detail. It'll be great, Meg! And I've even got the perfect name for it." She paused and then finished triumphantly. "Hello Jenny Week!"

Chapter

Meg could not believe what she was hearing.

"Well?" said Cricket, turning to her eagerly. "What do you think?"

"I . . ." But Meg didn't trust herself to speak. She saw one of the gerbils scratching at the side of its tank, and she knew exactly how it felt—trapped, with no way to escape. "But Cricket," she said, struggling to pull herself together. "I thought you said . . . I mean, didn't you tell Amy that this project was supposed to help someone?"

"Well, it is!" Cricket exclaimed. "It's helping *you,* silly!" She sounded as if she were explaining something perfectly obvious to someone who was sort of dim-witted. "Don't think I haven't noticed the way you've been acting lately. Every time one of us mentions Jenny, you get a funny look in your eyes. It's as if you're afraid we won't like her, or that her visit's going to be a total failure. You can't hide it, Meg. Not from friends like us. You're worried. It's written all over your face, even now."

"That's true," agreed Brittany, turning to Meg. "There have been a lot of times lately when I've thought something was bothering you. Only I figured it was because we were being . . . well . . . maybe a little too pushy."

Meg saw her chance. Now was the time to tell them. But what could she say? How could she explain now when Cricket was trying to help her? Before she could even begin to find the words she needed, Amy jumped in.

"Pushy? Us? What are you talking about, Brittany?" she said. "How could Meg think that? She knows we'll like Jenny and that we're dying to do things with her. We just haven't been very organized about it, that's all."

Meg saw Brittany cast a glance in her direction. She could feel her determination draining away. She looked at the clock above the chalkboard. It was almost dismissal time. Why couldn't the bell ring now? Then she could jump up and rush out of the classroom. She could run home and hide in her grandparents' house, not coming out, not answering the phone, not seeing any of them until she and Jenny returned from the cabin in the snow.

"Well, I suppose you're right, Amy," Brittany said, seeming to take Meg's silence for agreement. "I know we're going to like Jenny, and we should do everything we can to make her visit a success. My mother always says that if you plan things ahead of time, then you can relax and enjoy them when they come."

"That's exactly what my mother says!" declared Cricket. "In fact, that's how I came up with the idea. I was lying in bed last night, thinking about how lucky Meg was to have her Jenny coming, and how nice she must be. Not like my—" She stopped herself. "I mean"—she rushed on as if to cover up what had almost slipped out—"not like some people I know. Anyway, I was lying there thinking about how much fun Jenny's visit was going to be for all of us. And then I started thinking about Meg and how it wouldn't be much fun for her if she was as worried about it as she seemed. So I thought, why not do something that would make it possible for her to relax and enjoy things."

Meg tried to smile as Cricket beamed at her proudly, but it was difficult. The din in the classroom seemed to get louder. Out of the corner of her eye she saw the gerbil scratching harder. Maybe it had sensitive ears. If it hadn't been against Mr. Crockett's rules, she would have dropped a few gingerbread cookie crumbs into the tank to make the poor thing feel better. She wished that someone would toss her a

51

few crumbs right now—crumbs of sympathy, not gingerbread! But that wasn't likely to happen. None of her friends sitting there with such excited looks on their faces knew what was going on in her mind. Even if they did, she wasn't sure that it was sympathy she'd get!

Cricket was too carried away to notice either the gerbil's plight or Meg's. She turned eagerly to Brittany and Amy. "Now here's what I think we should do," she said. "Each of us should choose one day of Jenny's visit and be responsible for planning it out. You can think about it tonight. I've already got something planned," she added, smiling mysteriously, "though it may take up three days, not one. Anyway, we'll discuss our ideas at the meeting tomorrow. Nine o'clock, my house. My mother's already agreed. We can make up a master calendar. Meg could even use that computer program from her mom's company to print it out. Then we can spend next week making more detailed plans. We won't need to get together since we'll each be responsible for the day—or days— that we've chosen. Then when Jenny comes—"

Luckily, before she could say more, Mr. Crockett called the class to order so they could clean up the room. Meg was out of her seat in a flash. She'd never been more eager to clean up dirty plates and napkins.

Time. That's what she needed. Time to figure out how to tell them the truth. But she wasn't going to get it if she had to walk home from school with Cricket. She tossed a handful of paper plates decorated with pictures of candy canes and holly into the trash. As she did, she remembered something—the holly her grandmother had asked her to get on her way home from school. It was the perfect excuse.

"Boy, Meg, were you ever eager to clean up!" said Amy as the dismissal bell rang. She hurried after her, along with Brittany and Cricket, as Meg headed out of the classroom, down the hall crowded with laughing, shouting kids, and out the front door.

"The school should hire you as custodian," Cricket said. "Poor Mr. Birch would be out of a job."

Meg, planning her getaway, didn't comment. She saw the school bus Brittany rode waiting at the corner, and Amy's mother in her station wagon parked by the curb.

"Oh, good. She's here," Amy said, as her mother waved from the car. "She promised to take me Christmas shopping."

"Remember, tomorrow at nine," Cricket called as Amy ran down the steps.

"Don't worry," she shouted, getting into the car. "I'll be there!"

Brittany hesitated. "I have to go, too," she said. "I don't dare miss the bus. But . . . but are you all right, Meg? You haven't said much. I hope you don't think we're being too—"

"Of course she's all right," Cricket interrupted. "She's just overwhelmed by our generosity. Only kidding," she added quickly, grinning at Meg. "We're doing this for ourselves as much as for you. Right, Brittany? I just wish you could walk home with us. My mother's probably baking Christmas cookies."

Brittany made a face. "It's not fair," she said, seeming to forget about Meg. "I always miss out on things by riding the bus." The driver sounded the horn. "I'd better run. *A demain*," she called. "I mean . . . until tomorrow!"

Meg took a breath. This was her chance. "I've got to go, too," she said, moving quickly away from Cricket. "I have to stop at the florist to buy something for my grandmother. But you go on without me." She tried to sound casual as she headed down the crowded school steps to the sidewalk. "I wouldn't want you to miss those Christmas cookies."

"But Meg . . ." Cricket, looking confused, started after her. "Wait. What do you have to get?"

Meg walked faster. "Holly," she answered over her shoulder, wishing she could say something more important, like life-saving antibiotics, or a battery for her grandfather's pacemaker.

"Holly?" She heard the disbelief in Cricket's voice, then her footsteps pounding after her. "But you can't buy holly," Cricket said, grabbing her arm.

Anger suddenly bubbled up inside Meg. It was bad

enough having Cricket come up with this Hello Jenny project, but to hear her say she couldn't buy a bunch of holly for her grandmother . . . "Why not?" she demanded, pulling her arm away.

"Because I know where you can get it for free!" said Cricket, not paying any attention to her anger. And before Meg realized what was happening, she'd grabbed her by the arm again and was pulling her down the sidewalk in the opposite direction from town. "Don't worry. It's not far from here," she said. "But you'll have to be brave."

Meg saw a mischievous gleam come into Cricket's eyes and felt her anger dissolving. "What do you mean?" she said, curiosity taking its place. It was hard to stay angry with Cricket! "Where are we going?"

Cricket's face lit up. "To the witch's house!" she said. "Come on!"

Meg had no idea what she was talking about. What could she mean—a witch's house? She was teasing for sure, but at least she wasn't talking about Jenny, and it seemed easier to go along than to try to get away.

"Just wait until you see this," Cricket said. Then she clammed up, refusing to say another word—in spite of Meg's pleading—until they'd turned down a crooked little street that Meg had never noticed before.

"It's at the end of this block," announced Cricket. "Just one block from my house. That's how I know about it."

Meg didn't think this was the sort of block a witch would live on. The houses were neat, with carefully tended gardens and Christmas decorations on their windows and doors. She saw an old man raking leaves, a group of boys shooting baskets in front of a garage, and a woman shaking out a mop. There was nothing scary—until suddenly, looming out of a tangle of bushes and vines, she saw what Cricket meant.

It *was* a witch's house! Meg stared at the hulking, dark form. It was twice as large as the houses beside it, and it had a steeply peaked roof and a crooked chimney. Vines crawled up its walls, and its front lawn was nothing but a weed patch. Meg remembered a picture in a book she had about Baba Yaga, a Russian witch who lived in a house that stood on chicken legs. It wasn't hard to imagine this house suddenly jumping up and running off on skinny bird legs just like the house in that book did.

"Wow! Now I see what you mean," she said, shivering slightly.

Cricket looked pleased by her reaction. "Of course, a witch doesn't really live here," she said, heading for the hedge that surrounded the yard. "No one's lived here for ages, in fact. That's why we can sneak in and get the holly. There's an enormous bush of it in the backyard." She pushed aside part of the hedge, revealing a hole in the fence behind it.

Meg hesitated, thinking of Baba Yaga. "But should

we?" she said. "It's private property, even if no one lives here."

"I suppose," said Cricket. "But don't worry. I've done it lots of times." She squeezed through the hole in the fence. "Come on."

Meg's scruples, as well as her lingering fear of witches, were overcome by curiosity. Trying not to think of what would happen if anyone *did* live in the house, she followed Cricket, shoving the prickly hedge aside to squeeze through the hole and into the backyard.

The holly bush, ablaze with red berries and shiny green leaves, was the first thing she saw. It was more like a tree than a bush, and it filled one whole corner of the overgrown yard. Then Meg noticed an arbor covered with bare vines that might have been roses, a vast tangle of blackberry bushes, and scruffy trees of all sizes and shapes. Beneath everything was a carpet of unraked leaves. It was like the grounds of Sleeping Beauty's castle before the prince arrived.

"Isn't it something?" Cricket's voice fell to a whisper. "I always feel like I'm stepping into a fairy tale. See that gate?" She pointed to a rickety wooden gate at the rear of the yard. "It opens out on a pathway that cuts between the houses, straight across to my block. Jenny and I used to—" She stopped.

"Jenny?" Meg was on the alert again. But then she realized that Cricket couldn't mean her Jenny. "Do you mean *your* friend Jenny? The one who moved to Alaska?"

Cricket's face clouded over. For a moment it looked as if she wasn't going to speak. Then, just as Meg was about to repeat her question, she frowned and answered. "Yes. We used to come here all the time. We'd bring sandwiches and have picnics under the arbor. There are lots of blackberries here in the summer, and that's a plum tree." She pointed to a bare-branched tree opposite the holly bush. "The blossoms are beautiful in the spring, and later it's loaded with fruit. Jenny and I—" She stopped herself again. "Well . . . I guess you could say it was our own special place, but now . . ." She hesitated. "Now she's not my friend anymore," she declared, speaking to herself as much as to Meg. "Because if she was my friend, she'd write to me."

Meg was amazed. "You mean you haven't heard from her?" she said, thinking of how she'd feel if she hadn't heard from Jenny Snyder.

Cricket looked as if she didn't trust herself to speak.

From the telephone wires overhead a crow cawed loudly, and a car door slammed somewhere in front of the house. But Meg hardly noticed. She couldn't believe what she was hearing. No wonder Cricket had stopped talking about her Jenny. "You mean you haven't gotten even one little letter?" she said.

Cricket shook her head, then quickly corrected herself. "I did get a letter way back in August, after she first moved," she admitted. "I wrote back twice, but she never answered. I don't know why. I thought she was my friend, but now . . . I guess maybe I was wrong. I know I drive people crazy sometimes— getting all excited about things and talking too much. But I thought she . . . well . . . maybe that's why, when I realized that your Jenny was coming, I . . ." She hesitated.

Meg knew what she was going to say. She was going to try to explain that that's why she was so eager to make plans for Jenny's visit. She was going to get all teary-eyed and tell her that's why she wanted Hello Jenny Week to be a club project. Meg knew she should say something. She should tell Cricket how much she liked her, and she should say that Jenny could be her best friend, too. But the words wouldn't come out of her mouth.

She looked at the witch's house. Though it was still early, the sky was cloudy and the December afternoon light was starting to fade. The house looked more forbidding than ever. She noticed that paint was peeling from the frames around the darkened windows and the back porch slanted with age.

"It is pretty spooky, isn't it?" she said, changing the subject. She could tell Cricket was disappointed, but she made an effort not to show it.

"It's . . . it's better in the summer," she said, swallowing hard and turning away from Meg to look at the house. "Though I wouldn't want to live here even then," she added, her voice starting to regain some of its usual spirit.

"Neither would I," said Meg, shivering again slightly as she stared at the windows that watched them like eyes. She heard voices coming from somewhere, probably next door. "I can't imagine—"

"Meg!" Cricket suddenly grabbed her arm. Her long, thin fingers felt cold and tense. "Listen!"

All at once Meg heard a door slam, and then she heard voices. But they weren't coming from next door. They were coming from inside the house!

Suddenly a light went on, making the dust-covered windows shine like cats' eyes. "Oh no!" Cricket cried. "Someone's coming! Run!"

But they didn't.

Because even as Cricket spoke, the back door opened. And instead of a cackling, black-cloaked figure, a small blond-haired boy came out onto the porch. He looked across the yard at the two girls who were rooted to the ground as firmly as the holly bush, and his face broke out into a smile. "Meg!" he shouted, running down the steps as if it were the most natural thing in the world to find his sister standing there. "Come and see!" he cried. "We're going to live here. This is our new house!"

Chapter

Meg stared at her brother in astonishment. Her heart was pounding, her knees felt weak, and her brain was having a hard time taking everything in. What was Kevin doing here? And what had he just said?

"Our new house?" she repeated, looking down at his face, which was shining with excitement. Cricket's words—*I wouldn't want to live here!*—still rang in her ears.

"Yes!" exclaimed Kevin. He grabbed her hand as well as Cricket's and dragged them across the yard and up the slanting steps to the back porch. "Isn't it great?" he said. "Mommy says we can have a rabbit and maybe a dog. I'm going to get my old bed back and—"

"Kevin!"

Meg heard her mother's voice calling from inside the house. And then there she was, coming out the door and onto the back porch where Cricket, Meg, and Kevin were standing. She was followed by a man with sandy-colored hair and a freckled face. It was Tim Eliot, the real estate agent who'd been showing her houses, the one who'd found the fixer-upper that she'd left early this morning to see. Oh no, Meg thought, could this be—

"Meg! Oh my goodness!" Mrs. Kelly exclaimed, stopping in her tracks. "What are *you* doing here?"

"We . . . we came to get holly," said Meg. "But . . ." This couldn't be the house, she thought desperately. It had to be a mistake, or a joke, or some kind of dream. But if it was a dream, then what was her mother doing standing here with the real estate agent?

"We didn't mean any harm," Cricket said, coming to Meg's aid just as her grandmother, and then her grandfather, appeared in the doorway. "My friend and I . . . I mean, a girl I once knew, used to come here to play. We called it—" She stopped before she could say "the witch's house."

"Well, isn't this amazing!" exclaimed Grandma. "We were just at the school looking for you. Your mother left work early, then picked up Kevin, your grandfather, and me so she could show us this place. Of course, she wanted you to come, too."

"That's right," said Mrs. Kelly, still looking confused. "But I never expected—"

"Well, you know what they say," said Grandpa.

"Expect the unexpected, especially where these girls are concerned." He winked at Meg. "But let's not waste any more time. We're all here, that's the important thing. Now let's see your new house!"

Meg felt as if the ground—or rather, the rickety back porch—was crumbling under her. She heard Cricket draw in her breath. "Then it's true?" Meg said. "We are going to live here?"

"As soon as I get the paperwork finished," Tim Eliot answered. He put his hand on Mrs. Kelly's shoulder.

She looked pleased. And pretty. Meg remembered the excitement she'd heard in her mother's voice that morning when she'd said Tim had called, and all the time they'd spent together looking at houses. She felt Cricket's eyes upon her, and suddenly Meg wished she could just disappear.

"Of course, it doesn't look like much right now," Mrs. Kelly said, not seeming to notice the expression on Meg's face. "But we're lucky to get it. It's been vacant for ages, and Tim finally persuaded the owners to let us lease it with an option to buy it at the end of the year. It's an excellent price and all our rent money will go toward the down payment. It was very smart of him," she added. "But then he's always been smart." She paused, and Meg saw her grandparents exchange a knowing glance.

What did *that* mean? How did her mother know

Tim Eliot had always been smart? She narrowed her eyes as she stared at the real estate agent. They'd only lived in Redwood Grove for three months. That was hardly enough time to know much about anyone.

Tim smiled nervously and took his hand off her mother's shoulder. "Well, I don't know how smart I am," he said modestly. "But I think you're going to like living here. It has lots of potential."

"Especially your room." Mrs. Kelly smiled a bit too brightly at Meg. "Now come on." Turning away, she took Kevin's hand and headed back into the house. "I can't get over finding you girls here," she called over her shoulder. "But I'm glad that we did, because now I can give all of you the grand tour."

Meg wasn't sure her legs would move. She could feel Cricket beside her, probably itching to say something about Tim, but before she could get a chance, Meg managed to will herself forward. The next thing she knew, they were all walking down a dark hall and into a big musty-smelling room.

Meg's heart sank. She forgot about Tim as she stared at the room in dismay. What could her mother have been thinking, wanting to buy this house? How could she say they were lucky? This was obviously the living room, but it was hard to imagine anyone living here. The walls were dingy, the floor was bare, the windows were dirty, and the huge stone fireplace was covered with cobwebs and dust.

"Will you look at that," Cricket whispered. For a moment Meg thought she meant her mother and Tim, who were struggling side by side to open a window that was stuck. But it was the fireplace that had caught Cricket's eye. "It's like something out of a fairy tale, isn't it?" she said. "I can just picture a witch's cauldron bubbling away!"

Meg didn't trust herself to speak. Kevin was running around the empty room making tooting noises like a train, and she wanted to shout "Shut up!" Not just at Kevin, but at Cricket, her mother, everyone. They *couldn't* be going to live here.

"Now the first thing we'll do, Meg," her mother said briskly, giving up on the window, "is get this place cleaned up. Once the windows are washed and the floors are polished, it'll look a thousand times better. Then we can plan the painting and decorating. This is the kind of house where you have to use your imagination and see the possibilities. I was thinking of a nice off-white in this room, and then blue for the kitchen."

"Yes," called Grandma, who'd already made a quick inspection of the living room and was poking around in the kitchen, opening cabinets and peering into the pantry. "Blue would be perfect in here. I must say, Janet," she added approvingly, "you've done wonderfully well. This place is a real find. Just look at these details. They don't make houses like this anymore."

Meg bit her tongue. She wanted to say that she

could see why. But maybe it would be safer to just keep her mouth shut—at least until she was sure she could control what would come out of it. Besides, the kitchen actually was much better than the living room.

"Now this is more like it," Cricket said as they stepped inside. "It's not nearly so spooky. In fact, I'd say it's charming."

That wasn't exactly the word Meg would have used, but she had to admit that in spite of needing a paint job, the kitchen was bright, almost cheerful. It had a built-in china cabinet and there was a breakfast nook overlooking the lawn—or what would have been the lawn. It wasn't like the kitchen in Cricket's house, of course. That room had shiny countertops, sparkling windows, and French doors leading out to a garden filled with flowers and herbs. But Meg could see that with a fresh coat of paint and some prints on the walls, this room might look almost as good. Maybe that's what her mother meant about using her imagination. At least she could give it a try.

"Maybe you could make curtains, Mom," she ventured, regaining her voice. She didn't want to sound too enthusiastic, but she hated being such a spoilsport, especially when everyone else was looking at the good side of things. "Blue-and-white check," she suggested cautiously. "Or maybe yellow with some kind of flowers."

Mrs. Kelly looked relieved. "Good idea, Meg," she

said, exchanging a quick glance with Tim. He looked relieved, too. "I'm glad you're starting to see the possibilities. Now why don't you and Cricket go have a look at your room. It's right at the top of the stairs. It has a dormer window and . . . well, I'll let you see for yourself. Go on. I'll be up in a minute."

Cricket didn't need to be asked twice. "Come on," she said, taking the lead as they headed for the stairs. "Isn't this exciting? I mean, seeing the inside of this house after looking at it from the outside for so many years. Not that you've been looking at it for years, of course. I meant me and—" She stopped before she could say Jenny's name and quickly changed the subject. "Who is that real estate guy?" she said. "He's good-looking, isn't he? And your mother seems to—" She broke off when she saw the look on Meg's face. "Not that it's any of my business," she mumbled quickly, starting up the stairs.

But Meg wasn't about to let her go on. "Cricket, stop!" she commanded, catching up with her and grabbing her arm. This was her house, after all—even if she didn't much like it. And it was her room they were going to see. She wasn't going to let Cricket, with all her nosy speculations, beat her to it.

"Oh, right," said Cricket, looking embarrassed. "It's kind of like when we found the secret attic in your grandparents' house, isn't it? I didn't mean to take over. Go on."

Meg started up the stairs. She suddenly felt like a pot about to bubble over, but she wasn't going to let it happen, not now in this house with everyone here. She took a deep breath and tried to think of good things—like an attic. If this house had one, it might be full of treasures—old dolls, clothes, toys. She could explore it, maybe with Jenny if they had any time left when they got back from the snow. They wouldn't be living in the house yet, of course. It would take a long time to get it in shape. But her mother would have the keys. They could come over and search. Maybe they'd even find a secret staircase.

But as she reached the top of the stairs, Meg realized that there wasn't any attic—or rather that they were already in it.

"We're right up under the roof, aren't we?" said Cricket, looking at the steeply slanted ceiling. "This would be the attic if it hadn't been made into rooms." Then, forgetting about letting Meg go first, she opened the door at the top of the stairs.

"Wait! You can't do that!" Meg protested.

"Oops, sorry," Cricket apologized. "But it's only a bathroom." She stepped aside so that Meg could peer in. The long narrow room had an old-fashioned claw-footed tub in it. But there the resemblance to the lovely bathroom in Meg's grandparents' house stopped. This room had no stained glass window with lilies and irises. Instead, its fixtures were old and rusty, the tile was chipped, and the peeling wallpaper was covered with faded pink flamingos.

"Look at that awful paper!" Cricket exclaimed.

"Oh, I don't know. It's not so . . ." Meg began defensively. But there was nothing she could say in favor of the wallpaper. It *was* gruesome. Still, it was nothing compared to the paper that covered the walls of the room next door. "Oh no!" Meg groaned when she opened the door.

"Let me see!" Cricket peered over Meg's shoulder, and her eyes opened wide. "Wow!" she gasped. "I've never seen anything like that!"

Cautiously, almost holding their breath, the girls stepped into the room. Cowboys, horses, and long-horned steers stampeded wildly around them. It was a regular cattle drive! And under their feet, matching the colors of the livestock thundering over the tattered wallpaper, was a ratty, mottled brown rug.

Meg stared at the galloping cowboys and breathed in the musty odor—like the smell of wet dog—that rose from the carpet. Her spirits, which were already low, hit rock bottom. "Oh, Cricket," she moaned. "This is awful. What was my mother thinking? How could she have imagined I'd want a room like this?"

"Well, I don't think she meant the wallpaper," said Cricket tactfully. "But the ceiling is interesting, the way it slants and all. And you can put up new paper and get another rug. And look—" She pointed to the dormer window. "I'll bet that's what she was thinking of—a window seat!"

The moment Meg saw the window seat, she forgot about the wallpaper. She dashed across the musty rug, scarcely noticing the squishy feel beneath her feet. "Oh, I've always wanted one of these!" she exclaimed, sitting down on the wide wooden bench with drawers built in under it that stretched from one end of the dormer window to the other. It was easy to see the possibilities here. She could just imagine herself sitting at the window daydreaming, or looking at the sky on a starry night, or curling up to read on a rainy day. She'd need cushions, of course. Rose-colored, maybe. And lots and lots of throw pillows.

"Look, you can see my house from here," said Cricket, kneeling on the seat beside her and pointing out the window. She was right. Even though the panes were dirty, Meg could see the gate at the rear of the tangled garden, then the path, and in the distance Cricket's neat blue house. "We can send each other signals," Cricket said. "In Morse code!"

"Now there's an idea!" Mrs. Kelly poked her head into the room at just that moment. Meg had been so busy imagining her rose-colored cushions that she hadn't even heard her climbing the stairs. "So you've found it," her mother said now, smiling as she came into the room. "What do you think?"

"I think it more than makes up for the wallpaper

70

and the rug!" replied Meg. And then, before she realized what she was doing, she heard herself asking, "When can we move?" She was surprised at how quickly the question came out of her mouth. Only moments ago she would have been happy if the answer was never. But now, with this wonderful window seat, it all seemed different. "Of course, I know it'll take a while to get things ready," she added, not wanting to seem too impatient. "At least a month or two. Right?"

"A month or two? Are you kidding, Meg?" Mrs. Kelly shuddered at the idea. "I'm not about to wait that long. We've been camping out at your grandparents' house for too many months already. No, I plan to get this place cleaned up right away and move us in the week after Christmas."

Meg was on her feet in a flash. She forgot about throw pillows and rose-colored cushions. Those words—*the week after Christmas*—were the very same words she'd been repeating over and over to herself for the past month. "Mom, what are you talking about?" she said, crossing the room to confront her. "We can't move then. Not the week after Christmas. That's when Jenny's coming!"

Her mother frowned. "I know that, Meg," she said. "But—"

Meg didn't let her go on. "And what about the snow? Have you forgotten about that?" she said, forgetting that Cricket was right there, still kneeling on

71

the window seat. "The week after Christmas is when we're going to Lake Tahoe. To your friend's cabin. You, me, Kevin, and Jenny."

"What?"

Meg heard Cricket's startled question and saw her jump up from the window seat, but she didn't care. She stared at her mother in disbelief. She couldn't be saying that they'd have to give up the trip to the snow, the only time she and Jenny would have together. It wasn't fair! No window seat—not even one with rose-colored cushions—could make up for it. "Why do we have to move in here then?" she demanded. "Why not the week after?"

"Because the week after Christmas is the only time I can take off from work," Mrs. Kelly replied. "My boss told me today that I could take the week off, but then things are going to get hectic again. There will be sales conferences and a new project to start. I'd like to go on the snow trip, Meg. You know I would. But with just one week off I don't see how we'll have time. There'll be so much to do here and—"

She was interrupted by a shout from downstairs. "Janet, come help your father and me measure the living room. I think that rug we've got stored in the garage will—Kevin, wait!" Grandma's exclamation was followed by a loud crash.

"Oh no!" Mrs. Kelly exclaimed. "What's he up to now?" She started for the door.

72

"But, Mom," Meg protested.

"Look, Meg, we'll talk about this later," her mother said, as Kevin began to wail. "But I don't think it will be so bad for you to stay in Redwood Grove that week. You and Jenny will be able to spend more time with your friends." She headed down the stairs and was gone.

Meg turned to Cricket, realizing that she'd heard everything about the snow trip and her and Jenny going away for the week. "Listen, Cricket," she began. She had to explain things now. There was no avoiding it any longer. "I've been meaning to tell you—all of you—but somehow I just couldn't. You see, my mother has this friend who invited us to go to Lake Tahoe. But now we can't." She stopped as all the awfulness of it came rushing back to her. It was so unfair! After all her planning and all her work taking care of Kevin. She could hear him crying downstairs and she felt like doing the same thing—just throwing herself down on the window seat and letting the tears come out.

She was sure Cricket must be feeling the same way, but to her surprise Cricket didn't look angry or even upset. Just the opposite. "Oh, Meg!" she exclaimed, hurrying across the room and taking Meg's hands in hers. "This is incredible." Her eyes were shining with excitement. "It's kismet all over again!"

"What?" Meg didn't understand. What did kismet

have to do with it? "Do you mean that I'm destined to be unhappy?"

"Of course not," Cricket said. "This is something that's going to make you happy. Listen, I was going to tell you about it at the meeting tomorrow, when we were all talking about our ideas for Hello Jenny Week. But I think I'd better tell you now." She paused, then announced with a flourish, "You *can* go to the snow! That's my surprise. My dad said he'd take us there—to Lake Tahoe—for three whole days. You, me, Amy, Brittany, and Jenny. We'll rent a cabin and go skiing and tobogganing and ice skating. We'll drink hot chocolate and roast marshmallows. All five of us together! Won't that be great?"

Meg couldn't believe what she was hearing. It was awful. Terrible. Worse than anything she could have imagined. Meg thought of all the things Cricket had been saying—about the witch's house and how she wouldn't want to live there, about her mother and Tim and the wallpaper. Suddenly the pot that had been simmering inside her boiled over.

"No!" she snapped, pulling her hands away from Cricket as the cowboys and cattle thundered around them. "It wouldn't be great. I don't want to go to the snow with you and Amy and Brittany. I want to go with Jenny."

"But . . ." Cricket began, a startled look on her face. "What about Hello Jenny Week? I thought—"

"Well, you thought wrong," Meg declared angrily. She felt like she was on a bobsled racing out of control. She couldn't put on the brakes. "I don't need any help with Jenny's visit. And I can see why your Jenny hasn't written to you," she blurted out, the words flying from her mouth as if fanned by an evil spirit, maybe by the witch that had lived in this house. "She was probably glad to get away. If I moved, I wouldn't write to you, either!"

It was done. The words were out of her mouth and there was no calling them back. For a moment both girls were stunned. It was as if a lightning bolt had struck, plunging itself into the musty rug between them.

"I mean . . ." Meg began, feeling dazed as she realized what she'd said.

But Cricket had fled from the room.

"Wait!" Meg called helplessly. She heard Cricket's feet pounding down the stairs, and then the sound of the back door slamming shut. She rushed to the window seat, where just a few minutes before she and Cricket had been planning to send messages to each other. She peered through the dusty glass just in time to see Cricket, her head down, her hands to her face, dash across the overgrown lawn. She pushed open the gate at the rear of the yard and, without glancing back once, disappeared down the path.

Chapter

Meg didn't have time to think about what she should do. Before she could even turn away from the window, Kevin had climbed up the stairs and run in to show her the bandage on his knee.

"Mr. Eliot fixed it," he said proudly. "He's got first aid stuff in his car. He knows how to fix tires, too. And I can call him Tim if I want to."

As Meg was trying to absorb that bit of information—wondering suspiciously why Tim Eliot was trying to make friends with Kevin—Grandma and Grandpa came up the stairs and into the room. They oohed and aahed over the window seat, groaned about the wallpaper, and began making plans for stripping it off. Meg should have been interested, especially when her grandmother announced she would make a patchwork quilt to match whatever wallpaper pattern

Meg picked out, but she was too distracted to really listen until she heard her grandfather ask, "What happened to Cricket? Where did she go?"

"She . . . uh . . . she had to go home and feed Buster," Meg replied quickly. It was a lame explanation, but it was better than saying Cricket had gone home to clean her room, which was the only other excuse she could think of on such short notice. And it was much better than telling them what really had happened. Meg wasn't sure she'd ever be able to do that.

Luckily, before Grandma—who was harder to fool than Grandpa—could start prying, Meg's mother and Tim appeared to discuss plans for the bathroom and for Kevin's room. Kevin immediately latched onto Tim, who besides knowing how to fix tires and skinned knees, seemed to know all about knocking down walls and installing toilets. Grandma and Grandpa discussed rugs and drapes and paint colors. And soon everyone was too busy to ask any more questions about Cricket. In fact, by the time they all got in the car to drive home, no one—except Meg—seemed to remember that Cricket had even been there.

It was dinnertime before they pulled into the driveway at her grandparents' house in the redwoods. They'd dropped Tim Eliot off at his real estate office, stopped at a decorating store to borrow a book of wallpaper samples, and after a lot of muttering from

Grandpa about fat and preservatives, picked up a pizza for supper. The smell of tomato sauce, pepperoni, and cheese wafted from the box as they climbed the steps to the porch and opened the door.

"It's too bad about Cricket dashing off like that," said Grandma. The armful of holly that she piled up on the hall table must have reminded her that someone was missing. "She could have come back here and had pizza with us."

Meg heard what she said, but she didn't reply. She'd already headed into the study to check the answering machine. Cricket might have called. She'd been thinking about it all the way home. Maybe she'd gotten back to her house with its pretty gardens and cheery kitchen, and after Buster had jumped up and planted a slobbery kiss on her nose, she'd suddenly realized that she'd been in the wrong, too. Maybe she'd decided to apologize for the way she'd been planning to take over Jenny's visit, or at least to tell Meg that she didn't blame her for what she had said.

Meg's heart leaped when she saw the red message light blinking. Suddenly nervous, she rushed to the answering machine, pressed the replay button, and braced herself for what she might hear. But the voice that came out of the machine wasn't Cricket's. And it didn't belong to any of her grandparents' bird-watching friends, either. It was Jenny!

Meg sank into her mother's desk chair, feeling

relieved. If there was one person in all the world she wished she could talk to right now, it was Jenny.

"Hello, Meg, it's me, Jenny. Are you there?" Jenny's recorded voice said from the speaker. "Well, I guess not." She sounded disappointed, and suddenly a terrible thought flashed through Meg's mind. Maybe Jenny wasn't coming! Why else would she be calling on a weekday afternoon when the rates were so high? Something must have happened. Meg was so overcome by the thought that she almost missed Jenny's next words.

"You're probably wondering why I'm calling now," Jenny went on. "It's because I've got the most exciting news, and I couldn't wait to tell you! But now I guess I can't because you're not there, and I'm going to spend the night at my cousin's house so—Yes, Mom, I know! Listen, Meg, I can't stay on the line any longer. My mother says it costs too much, and anyway we're ready to leave. So bye, Meg, or whoever's listening to this. I'll call back tomorrow."

And that was it. Meg heard the beep that signaled the end of the message, and then the three beeps that meant there was nothing else on the tape. She stared at the red light glowing steadily from the machine's control panel. She wanted to pick up the machine and shake it like a piggy bank until more bits of information dropped out. How could Jenny be so cruel? Why didn't she just tell her the news, whatever it was? Why make her wait until tomorrow? She was dragging out the suspense, that's what she was doing. Just like . . .

Meg thought of Cricket. Maybe the two of them—Jenny and Cricket—were more alike than she'd realized. She thought of how excited Jenny's voice had sounded, of how her words had tumbled out, practically bumping into each other as they leaped off the tape. Wasn't that just like Cricket? And weren't they both full of interesting ideas and always ready for fun? Of course, she reminded herself, Jenny was a lot more understanding than Cricket, and better at solving problems, too—especially between friends. Or maybe it just seemed like that because she lived so far away. In fact, now that Meg thought of it, she and Jenny had had their share of fights, too. Quite a few of them actually. They didn't *always* get along.

Without thinking, she picked up the phone and began to punch in Cricket's number. They had to make up, just as she and Jenny always had. She knew exactly how the conversation should go. She'd say she was sorry and ask Cricket to forgive her. Then Cricket would say . . . but maybe she wouldn't. Meg stopped punching in numbers. What if Cricket wasn't like Jenny? After all, she hadn't apologized yet, though she'd had plenty of time. She could have called and left a message on the answering machine just as Jenny had done. Maybe it would be better to wait, Meg thought. Because if she apologized and Cricket didn't, she might get angry all over again! She put down the receiver, glad that at just that moment, Kevin burst into the study to tell her the pizza was getting cold.

Mrs. Kelly looked at Meg curiously when she came out of the study. "Was that Jenny's voice I heard on the machine?" she asked. "Or Cricket's?"

"It was Jenny's," Meg replied quickly. "She had some kind of news, but she didn't say what it was. She's going to call back tomorrow."

Mrs. Kelly didn't look entirely satisfied. But it wasn't until later, when Kevin was in bed, Grandma and Grandpa were watching a nature show on TV, and Meg was sitting beside her on the living room sofa looking at wallpaper samples that she finally said, "I know it's none of my business, Meg, but I have a feeling something's happened between you and Cricket. If you want, we can talk about it."

Meg quickly shook her head. She'd spent the whole evening trying to put Cricket out of her mind, and she didn't want to let her in now. Maybe tomorrow she could talk, when she was sure she'd cooled down. But not tonight.

"Well, I'm sure it'll all work out," her mother said. "Things always do. Like the house." She paused. "I know it was a shock to you, Meg. And I also want you to know how very sorry I am about not being able to go on the snow trip. But maybe, if we all work hard, we could manage a day or two."

Meg suddenly remembered Cricket's plan for three whole days at Lake Tahoe. She pushed it out of her mind and concentrated on the wallpaper pattern spread out across her lap. Baskets of spring flowers alternated with bluebirds and butterflies. Grandma could probably copy the pictures to appliqué on the quilt she'd promised to make for Meg's new room. Maybe she could make matching pillows for the window seat, too. She looked up at her mother. Somewhere between the decorating store and the pizza parlor they'd arrived at a temporary truce. Now it was time to make it permanent.

"Don't worry, Mom," she said, not wanting to fight with anyone anymore. "If we can't go, we can't go. Jenny will understand. I'll tell her when I talk to her tomorrow," she added, hoping that Jenny's big news wasn't going to be that she was getting ice skates or skis for Christmas. "And . . . and I am glad about the house. It'll be nice to get our furniture back. I'm sure it's going to look fine, once we get it fixed up."

"Oh, Meg." Mrs. Kelly's eyes suddenly grew moist. "You don't know how happy that makes me," she said, giving Meg a squeeze. "I've been so worried about everything. This house is a big responsibility. I know it's going to be a lot of work, but I'm sure we can make something of it. And we don't have to actually move in while Jenny's here. We can have our furniture delivered and sleep at Grandma and Grandpa's until everything's set up. Tim's going to help me find someone to clean up the yard and fix the plumbing and—" She stopped, and looked at Meg cautiously. "That's something else I wanted to talk to you about," she said.

"The plumbing?" Meg, who'd been thinking about Jenny getting ice skates and wondering if there was an indoor rink anywhere near Redwood Grove, thought of the bathroom with the flamingo wallpaper. But chipped tiles and rusty pipes weren't what her mother had in mind.

"No, not that," she said. "I mean Tim."

Meg felt a sudden draft as the wind whistled down the chimney, out of the fireplace, and into the living room, blowing cold ashes onto the carpet. Her grandfather must have forgotten to close the flue. "Did you say Tim?" she asked, hoping she hadn't heard right. But at the same time she remembered how his hand had looked resting on her mother's shoulder. "What about him?"

"Well . . ." Mrs. Kelly hesitated. She glanced down at the wallpaper book as if trying to compose herself. "Well, I just wanted to tell you, Meg, that even though I've found a place for us to live now, Tim and I may still go out together sometimes. Not house hunting, of course, but to the movies or dinner—things like that."

"You mean dates?" Meg forgot about Jenny and Cricket and the wallpaper samples as she stared at her mother.

"Well, is that so awful?" said Mrs. Kelly. "You make it sound like going to the dentist. Tim's really very nice," she continued, the shadow of a smile playing around her lips. "He's kind and he's smart. He has a good sense of humor, and—"

"But Mom," Meg interrupted, stopping her mother before she could go on listing all of Tim Eliot's good traits. She was making him sound like an Eagle Scout, or a golden retriever. "You can't rush into these things," she said. She couldn't help noticing that she sounded a bit like her grandmother. "You hardly know him."

"Oh, I wouldn't say that," Mrs. Kelly murmured.

All at once, Meg remembered the look that had passed between her grandparents when her mother had mentioned that Tim had always been smart. "What do you mean by that, Mom?" she said suspiciously. "Something's going on, isn't it?" Her voice rose and she twisted around on the sofa, knocking the wallpaper book to the floor.

Her mother held up her hand. "Calm down, Meg," she said. "There's really nothing to tell. It's just that . . . well, you know that senior prom?"

"Senior prom?" Meg echoed. What was her mother talking about? Then suddenly she remembered the conversation in the hall that morning when her mother had gotten defensive about the almost-strapless dress and wanting to stay out until dawn. And all at once she knew what her mother was going to say. "You mean Tim . . ." she began.

Her mother nodded. "Yes. We went to Redwood Grove High School together. And Tim was my date to the prom!"

C h a p t e r

Sleep didn't come easily for Meg that night. How could it when she'd just found out her mother had a secret life. Or at least, a life that Meg didn't know anything about. She wondered what else her mother hadn't told her. Maybe it was better not to know!

She tossed and turned, waking up at midnight to think about Jenny and the message she'd left on the answering machine. Whatever her news was, it had to be good because she'd sounded so excited. Maybe she was going to be able to stay in Redwood Grove longer than a week. Or maybe her parents had won the lottery, though if they had, her mother probably wouldn't have been worried about a phone call costing too much.

She woke up again at three, this time to think about Cricket. She remembered the expression on her face when Meg had allowed those terrible words to fly out of her mouth. How could she have done it? How could she have told Cricket that her friend was glad to get away from her? It had been awful then and it seemed even worse now as she thought about it, lying in bed in the dark of the night. Cricket's actions hadn't been anywhere near as bad as Meg's words. She'd been pushy perhaps, with all her efforts to make Jenny's visit a success, but at least her heart was in the right place. She hadn't wanted to hurt anyone, which was more than Meg could say for herself. Staring up at the ceiling while the whole world slept, she faced what deep in her heart she'd known all along. *She* was the one who'd have to apologize, because Cricket had nothing to apologize for. It would be hard, but she had to do it. She'd call Cricket first thing in the morning, the moment she woke up.

The good feeling that always seemed to come from doing the right thing—or even from planning to do the right thing—flowed through Meg. She closed her eyes and didn't open them again until the dial on the clock by her bed read 9:25. It wasn't the clock that awakened her, though. It was Amy and Brittany.

She heard them first in the downstairs hallway, talking to her mother. Then as she sat up in bed, rubbed the sleep from her eyes, and glanced at the clock, she heard them pounding up the stairs. They burst into her room just as she remembered that it was Saturday and the meeting Cricket had called was scheduled—or had been scheduled—to start at nine.

Brittany was the first one through the door. "Meg, where were you?" she cried breathlessly. She had a stricken look on her face. Meg noticed that one of Brittany's hands was clenched tightly shut, as if she were holding something inside it.

Amy marched across the room after her. "No, that's not the question," she said, glaring down at Meg. "The question is, what did you say to her?"

Meg groaned. She knew right away what Amy meant. "Oh no! Did Cricket tell you?" she said. "But it was all a mistake. I was just so upset. I'm going to apologize. I'm going to call her right now." She flung her comforter aside and leaped out of bed. But Amy stopped her.

"Don't bother," she said. "It won't do any good. She's already gone."

"That's right," Brittany added. She looked nervously at Amy and anxiously at Meg. "Her family left early for Fresno. When we got there they were putting the last of their suitcases into the car. Cricket said she was canceling the meeting and that you would know why. She said we could hold one if we wanted to, but—" She stopped as if she couldn't bear to go on. Meg saw her fingers close more tightly around what she was holding. "She said . . ." she began again hesitantly.

"Oh, come on, Brittany," Amy interrupted. "Just say it. Cricket is quitting the club!"

Meg felt as if the floor had suddenly fallen out from under her. She stared at Amy. "But . . . but that can't be true," she said. Even in the darkest hours of the middle of the night she'd never imagined it could come to anything like this. "You must have heard wrong. Cricket loves the Always Friends Club. She never would quit!"

"Oh yes she would," said Amy angrily. "And she has." She turned to Brittany. "Show her," she said.

Brittany, looking thoroughly miserable, opened her hand. Lying in her palm was a small silver-colored heart engraved with the words *Always Friends* and beneath them *Cricket.*

Meg's own heart nearly stopped as she stared at the shiny piece of metal. She took it from Brittany's hand. She had one just like it, of course, engraved with her own name. Cricket had bought a heart for each of them after they'd finished the project that helped her get Buster. Buster had one, too, in fact, since they were actually dog ID tags.

Her fingers closed over the metal, still warm from Brittany's hand. She'd known Cricket was hurt—how could she not be?—but she'd never expected this.

Suddenly, feeling Cricket's heart digging into the palm of her hand, and Brittany's and Amy's eyes upon her, the whole story tumbled out. Meg told them everything—about Jenny and the snow trip, about the witch's house and the wallpaper, even about her mother and Tim. And then she told them what she'd said to Cricket.

For a moment, after the torrent of words had stopped, none of the girls said anything. Meg had been hoping that when she finished speaking, they'd jump to her defense and tell her that what she had said wasn't really so bad. But they didn't. Instead, Amy stared at her as if she couldn't believe her ears. Then as the words sunk in, she let out a groan and flopped down on the bed.

"Well *that* was pretty awful," she said, dashing Meg's hopes. Meg supposed she should be grateful that she didn't storm out of the room and quit the club, too. "I've been annoyed with Cricket myself sometimes, but I never would have said anything like that!"

"But Amy," Brittany protested, seeing the look on Meg's face. "Meg was upset—about moving to a new house with all that awful wallpaper, and about her mother and this Tim guy. I knew we were being too pushy about Jenny's visit. Didn't I say so? If only you'd told us how you felt, Meg."

"I wanted to," said Meg miserably, sinking down on the bed beside Amy. "But it seemed so selfish of me," she tried to explain. "You were all so excited about Jenny coming, and you'd helped earn the money for her plane ticket."

"But we've all helped each other," said Brittany.

"We've each gotten a share of the club earnings, so you were only spending what was rightfully yours. As for wanting to have some time alone with Jenny . . . well, there's nothing wrong with that, is there, Amy? Just because we're friends doesn't mean we have to do everything together."

Amy seemed to be softening. She had a quick temper, but she never stayed angry for long. "No, of course not," she said. "Look at all the time I spend with my soccer team. And Brittany has her riding lessons, and Cricket—" She stopped. The three girls looked at each other. Meg knew they were thinking the same thing.

"We've *got* to get her back," she said, jumping up from the bed again. She paced to the window and back, running her fingers through her tangled hair. "I'll apologize the second she returns from Fresno," she promised. "Maybe she'll have calmed down by then, what with Christmas and everything."

"Maybe. But I wouldn't count on it," Amy warned. "She's felt bad for months about not hearing from Jenny. What you said was like turning a knife in a wound." Meg winced at her choice of words. "I don't think she'll just forget about it, no matter how many great presents she gets for Christmas. And I don't think any ordinary kind of apology will work. Do you, Brittany?"

Brittany cast a sympathetic glance at Meg and sat

down on the bed beside Amy. "I don't think so," she admitted. "She was pretty upset. I can see why, too. It wasn't just what you said, Meg, but what she was already feeling. The thing I don't understand is why her friend hasn't written. You knew her, Amy. Did she seem like the sort of person who'd just disappear?"

Amy shook her head. "No. And she really liked Cricket, so I'm sure it's not that she was glad to get away from her." Meg winced again, remembering what she had said. "I suppose something could have happened to her, though," Amy went on. "She moved to Alaska. That's a pretty wild place, isn't it? She could have fallen off a glacier or gotten eaten by a polar bear. Just kidding," she added quickly, as Brittany opened her mouth to protest.

But Meg was nodding in agreement. "You could be right, Amy," she said. "I don't mean about glaciers and polar bears. But something else could have happened to her. She might have gotten sick or had an accident."

"Or she might have moved again," said Brittany, who didn't like to think about bad things happening to people. "Maybe none of Cricket's letters got through. Or she might have put off writing for so long that now she's embarrassed and doesn't know how to start again. I know that's how I'd feel. If only we had an address, or a phone number so we could call her. Didn't she ever write to you, Amy?"

"Just once," Amy said. "She sent me a postcard

right after she moved. I'm sure I've still got it at home somewhere. It didn't have a return address on it, but . . ." She frowned and closed her eyes as if trying to visualize the postcard. "But I think . . . yes! It had a picture of the town she moved to. I don't remember the name, but that must be on the card, too." She turned to Meg excitedly. "You know, I think all we'd have to do to find her is get a phone book for that town—it was a small sort of place. Then we can look up Wozniak— that's Jenny's last name. There probably aren't too many people named that."

"You're right!" said Brittany. "And we wouldn't even need a phone book. If we had the name of the town, we could call information and they'd give us the number. Then we could phone her. What do you think, Meg? Are you willing to do it?"

For the first time since Amy and Brittany had burst into her room, Meg felt her spirits rising. Maybe they were right. Maybe they could find Cricket's Jenny and get her to call or to write. Then Cricket would have to forgive Meg, wouldn't she?

Of course, there were a lot of things that could go wrong. Jenny's family might have an unlisted number, or they might have moved from the town on Amy's postcard. But it was certainly worth a try. They had nothing to lose. And it might be the only way of getting Cricket back in the club.

"What I think is that I'd better get dressed," she

said, heading for her closet as she answered Brittany's question. She heard the phone in her grandparents' room across the hall ring and then her grandmother's voice answering it, but she was too busy making plans to pay much attention. "We'll go to Amy's house first and find that postcard," she said, grabbing a pair of jeans and a sweatshirt. "Then we can—"

But before she could say what they would do next, she heard her grandmother call, "Meg!" She came into the room, the cordless phone in her hand. "It's for you," she said, handing the phone to Meg. "It's Jenny!"

For a moment all Meg could think of was Alaska. Had their thoughts been so powerful that they'd traveled over thousands of miles without benefit of phone lines? Did Cricket's friend have some kind of extrasensory perception? Then as she took the phone from her grandmother's hand, she realized who she'd meant. It was *her* Jenny calling, not Cricket's.

"Do . . . do you want us to leave?" asked Brittany hesitantly, getting up from the bed. Meg's grandmother was already gone. "We can wait downstairs," she said, glancing toward the door. "I mean, if you'd rather not have us around while you're talking to Jenny."

Meg looked at Brittany and Amy and felt a lump rise in her throat. Just yesterday that would have been exactly what she wanted. But now . . . "No, stay," she said. "Please. You're *all* my best friends—Cricket, too. And I've got so much to tell Jenny, I'll probably need

95

help!" She dropped the clothes she was holding, then sat down on the blanket chest at the end of her bed and put the phone to her ear.

"Hello, Jenny? Oh, I'm so glad you called!" she exclaimed as she heard Jenny's voice. "You're not going to believe what's been happening. I don't know where to begin, so I'll just—"

"Meg, wait!" Jenny's voice came over the line so loudly that Amy and Brittany, who'd crowded around Meg, jumped back and Meg herself had to hold the phone away from her ear. "Didn't you get my message? Don't you want to know my news? Oh, I wish Cricket was there," she rushed on. "She's not, is she? I thought I heard someone talking. Is it her?"

"Uh . . . no," replied Meg, feeling confused. What was Jenny getting at? "Amy and Brittany are here," she explained, "but not Cricket. In fact, Cricket's one of the things I was going to tell you about."

"Then this must be extrasensory perception!" exclaimed Jenny. "Or maybe some of that kismet stuff. Because Cricket's the reason *I'm* calling you! Well, not the whole reason, but . . . listen, are you sitting down, Meg?"

"Yes, but—"

"I'm just asking," Jenny interrupted, her voice crackling with excitement, "because you're going to be in for a shock. I nearly fell down myself when I heard it." She paused.

Meg could just picture her drawing in a breath, trying to calm down. "Jenny, what is it?" she said impatiently. "Tell me."

"Okay," Jenny said. "Here goes. Yesterday at choir practice I met someone who used to live in Redwood Grove! And guess who she is?" She didn't wait for an answer. "She's that friend of Cricket's that you told me about when you first moved up there. The one with the same first name as me. Jenny! Jenny Wozniak."

Meg dropped the phone. It slid right out of her hand as if it had been greased with butter.

"Meg, what is it?" cried Brittany, scrambling to pick the phone up from the floor where it had fallen.

"You look like you've just seen a ghost!" said Amy.

"I . . . I . . ." Meg's voice stuck in her throat.

"Meg?" Jenny shouted over the line. "Are you there?"

"Yes." Meg took the phone from Brittany and held it to her ear. Her fingers were trembling. "But . . ." Her voice returned, but she didn't feel as if she could speak, at least not in any way that would make sense. "Jenny, listen," she said. "I'm going to get Amy and Brittany to pick up on the other extensions. I don't think I can handle this all by myself!"

Amy and Brittany raced down the stairs. Amy picked up the phone in the study, while Brittany grabbed the phone from the downstairs hall table. With everyone on the line, the rest of Jenny's phone call turned into a four-way conversation. At first it wasn't easy to make sense of things, with everyone asking questions and talking at once, but finally they managed to calm down and the whole story came out.

It wasn't a happy one, because it turned out that what had happened to Jenny—Cricket's Jenny whom Meg's Jenny had just met—was that her parents had split up a month after they'd moved to Alaska. Now she and her mother were living in Los Angeles with relatives. She hoped that her parents would get back together, and in fact, she and her mother were returning to Alaska to see her father for Christmas.

"Well, no wonder she didn't write," said Amy when Jenny finished telling her story. "She must have been out of her mind with worry."

"She was," said Jenny. "Of course, I just met her so I don't know all that much about it, but when it came out that I know Cricket . . . well, I don't really know her, but I feel like I do. Anyway, when Cricket's name came up, she got all teary-eyed and said she felt awful because she hadn't stayed in touch. So I thought—"

Meg couldn't keep still any longer. She had to interrupt to tell *her* story. And once she got started, it all came out. She told Jenny everything—all about the house her mother had found, and the snow trip that had been canceled, and the cowboy wallpaper, and the fight she'd had with Cricket, and finally what Cricket had done when Amy and Brittany showed up for the meeting.

"What?" Jenny broke in, when she got to that part. "She quit the Always Friends Club? But you can't let her do that!"

"We're not going to," said Meg.

"Not if we can help it," said Brittany. "Oh, Jenny. If only *her* Jenny could fly up here with you next week. If Cricket could just see her . . ."

"That's exactly what I was thinking!" said Jenny. "Of course, she can't actually fly up with me because she's going to visit her dad. But I've got an idea that's almost as good." As Brittany, Amy, and Meg listened, she outlined her plan. "Well?" she said when she'd finished. "Do you think it will work?"

"Oh, Jenny." Meg pressed the cordless phone to her ear, wishing that Jenny were here in her room so she could throw her arms around her. "Yes! I think it will."

"I *know* it will!" said Brittany.

"It's got to!" said Amy.

"Good. Then I'll do it," Jenny declared. "As soon as I can borrow the equipment from my uncle. Now I've got to hang up. This phone call's going to cost me a whole month's allowance. And Meg, don't feel bad about us having to stay in Redwood Grove for the week," she added. "I'd love to work on your new house. We can hang wallpaper. I know how to do it because I helped my mother paper our bathroom. We can make covering up that cattle drive an Always Friends Club project!"

Chapter

Meg could never remember a week going by as slowly as the one that followed the conversation with Jenny. Not that there wasn't plenty to do. Besides getting ready for Christmas—with all the usual shopping, tree decorating, and cookie baking—Amy and Brittany had leaped at Jenny's idea of getting Meg's new house ready to live in.

"She's right. It's a perfect club project," Amy had said when they'd hung up their phones and gathered in Meg's room again. "And there's no sense waiting to begin. We can do a lot before Jenny gets here. Then, if her plan works and if Cricket decides—I mean *when* Cricket decides to come back to the club—we can finish things up together. We'll wallpaper your room and maybe we'll even have time to go to the snow—if Cricket's dad is still willing to take us, that is."

Meg didn't even want to think about that. If they could just get Cricket back, if Cricket would just stop hating her, that would be enough. She could see that Brittany, who was more of a worrier than Amy, was thinking the same thing.

"*Oui* . . . I mean, yes," Brittany agreed, slipping for a moment into French. "A snow trip would be a nice thing to do, but let's not count on it. For now let's just work on the house."

So they did. All the next week—in spite of relatives coming to Amy's house with little cousins to be cared for, and parties being given at Brittany's house with guests to be entertained—both girls showed up for at least a few hours each day to help Meg and her family get their new house in order. They wore jeans and sweatshirts and got tired and grubby working outdoors raking leaves, and indoors scrubbing woodwork and sweeping cobwebs. Meg's mother hired a team of gardeners with chain saws and mowers to tame the overgrown yard. Meg's grandparents scraped chipped paint from window frames, oiled squeaky door hinges, replaced rusted drawer pulls, and took turns taking care of Kevin so he wouldn't get underfoot.

And Tim Eliot dropped by whenever he could. He painted the kitchen with Meg's grandfather, and the living room with her grandmother, and showed Meg and her friends how to strip the cowboy wallpaper off the walls so that Meg's room would be ready for repapering with butterflies, bluebirds, and spring flower baskets.

"Any time you girls want to go into the house restoring business just let me know," he said the day before Christmas Eve, when they'd finally finished the last of the stripping and were sweeping up the room. He was wearing a suit and tie because he'd stopped by on his way to Mrs. Kelly's office. She was taking him to her company's Christmas party.

He grinned at Meg, who'd put down her broom to try out the cushions her grandmother had bought for the window seat. They were plain white cotton, but she'd promised to cover them with rose-colored velveteen. "What do you think of this place now?" he asked. "Was I right about it having potential?"

What could Meg say? Her room—indeed the whole house—had obviously been loaded with potential, though she hadn't been able to see it herself. Now, even without the new wallpaper that was stacked up in neat rolls waiting to be hung, the room looked a thousand times better. The musty old rug was gone, heaved into the Dumpster full of junk that was parked in the driveway, ready to be hauled away. The windows and the woodwork were clean, and a new rug had been ordered. It would be delivered on Wednesday, along with Meg's bed and her doll house, and all the other furniture that had been in storage ever since they'd moved to Redwood Grove.

Meg could hardly wait to see how the house would look filled with their familiar chairs and sofas, tables and pictures. Of course, there was plenty of work still to be done—things like fixing the bathrooms and the back porch and the sink in the kitchen, plus more wall-papering and painting. It would take months for the grounds to begin to look pretty with freshly planted flowers, new shrubbery, and grass. And now that the thick covering of vines had been removed, it was clear that the outside of the house needed a good coat of paint. But at least it didn't look like a witch's house anymore. No one would expect Baba Yaga to leap out the door.

"I think it's turned out really well," she said, smiling at Tim and thinking to herself—though she wasn't quite ready to say it to anyone else—that *he* had turned out pretty well, too. "Thanks for helping us," she added.

"My pleasure," Tim replied, grinning again. "Now I'd better get going or I'll be late for that party. Hope you girls have a Merry Christmas. And remember, Meg," he said, "I'm invited for dinner so I'm counting on you to keep an eye on your grandfather. I want a real turkey and no tofu in the mashed potatoes, please!"

Brittany sighed as Tim disappeared down the stairs. "What a nice guy, Meg," she said. "And such a romantic story. Just the sort of thing Cricket would—" She stopped and looked at Meg and Amy seriously.

"You know we've got to decide what to do," she said. "She'll be back from Fresno the day after Christmas. Should we call her, or stop by her house? Or should we just go to the airport to pick up Jenny without her?"

Meg, who'd been waking up in the middle of the night thinking about exactly the same thing, didn't know what to say. She was sure that Cricket was still angry. Otherwise she would have called at least one of them from Fresno. "I don't know," she said. "I'm afraid that if I phone her she'll hang up. And I'm sure that if I go over to her house she'll slam the door in my face."

"What I think," said Amy, emptying her dustpan into the trash, "is that we shouldn't do anything about Cricket until Jenny gets here. That way we won't waste time or take any chances. We'll put the full plan into effect, and if she's still angry then, well . . . good riddance, I say!"

Meg was certain she didn't mean it. Amy would never write off Cricket that quickly. But she wasn't about to disagree. The last thing the club needed was another argument! "All right," she said. "We'll forget about Cricket for now. The three of us will go to the airport and put the plan into action as soon as we get back."

"Terrific!" said Amy. "I'll bring the sign I made."

"And I'll bring my camera," said Brittany, who'd been keeping a photographic record of all the changes they'd made to Meg's house. "That is . . . if you're sure you want us to go with you," she added.

"Of course I do! I can't imagine you *not* going!" said Meg. And she meant it. "Only you've got to be ready on time. I'm going to make my mother leave at least two hours early so we'll be absolutely sure to be there when Jenny's plane comes in."

She wasn't kidding. The sun had barely come up Monday morning when Meg jumped out of bed, already worried about being late. She didn't stop worrying about it until they were all safely in the car and her mother had driven across the bridge and through the city, pulling into the parking lot of the San Francisco airport a full hour before Jenny's flight was due in. There was plenty of time to get a good parking spot, even though the airport was crowded with holiday travelers. After finding out which gate Jenny's plane would arrive at, Mrs. Kelly settled down with a newspaper while Meg, Amy, and Brittany checked out the souvenir stands and candy machines and read the travel posters.

"Maybe we can all take a trip together sometime," Brittany said. "We could earn the money for it by doing lots of club projects."

"That would be great," agreed Amy. "I'd like to go to Hawaii, or maybe Australia. We could go snorkeling on the Great Barrier Reef. I saw a show about that on TV. You wouldn't believe all the beautiful fish you can see. How about you, Meg?"

But Meg was too nervous to think about tropical

vacations. The moment they'd hit the airport her imagination had started working double-time. They'd gotten here early, but what if Jenny had overslept and not made it to the Los Angeles airport in time? What if the pilot had overslept, or the plane ran out of fuel, or the landing gear got stuck? Announcements kept coming over the airport public-address system, but the only words she could catch were "white courtesy telephone, please." Suppose Jenny had left her a message? Suppose she'd missed hearing her name?

"Will you stop fidgeting," Amy said as they sorted through a collection of T-shirts in the souvenir shop. "I'm sure nothing's happened."

"Yes," Meg said, "but . . ."

Brittany shot her a sympathetic glance. "I know. Let's check the arrival time again," she suggested. "People always think planes are late, but sometimes they get in early."

Meg leaped at the idea. Brittany had done a lot of traveling, so maybe she was right. Besides, it would be better than standing here looking at stupid T-shirts with pictures of cable cars on them. She followed Brittany and Amy out of the shop. She knew she was being foolish, of course. Jenny had probably gotten to the airport an hour early, just as she had. And planes didn't run out of fuel except in the movies.

"Sorry for being such a worrywart," she said as they came to a halt in front of the bank of monitors displaying departure and arrival times. "It's just that—oh no! Look!" she exclaimed, as her eyes scanned the list of flight numbers glowing from the monitors. "You were right, Brittany. Her flight is early!"

All at once, after having had so much time to spare, everything was squeezed into a few minutes. The girls raced through the airport concourse and back to the gate, nearly knocking over a cart full of suitcases and bumping into a security guard. Luckily, he didn't think they were hijackers, and after warning them to slow down, he waved them into the gate area. Mrs. Kelly was already standing with a crowd of other people, waiting for the passengers to come up the ramp from the plane. She waved when she saw the girls and motioned for them to hurry as the voice over the loudspeaker announced, "Flight 117 from Los Angeles has arrived at Gate 23."

Amy paused just long enough to grab her sign from under the chair where Mrs. Kelly had been sitting. It was made out of poster board with the words HELLO, JENNY! printed across it in big bold letters. She held the sign aloft as Brittany adjusted her camera and Meg hurried past her mother to the front of the crowd. The passengers were already appearing. A mother, hurrying to catch up with a toddler who'd broken away from her grasp, came first. Then an older couple carrying tennis rackets, a family wearing Mickey Mouse ears from Disneyland, a young man with a garment bag. And then, there she was. Jenny!

For a moment, Meg couldn't move. Time seemed to stand still. How alive Jenny looked! For months she'd been picturing her in two dimensions, as she appeared in the photograph tacked to her bulletin board. Now here she was in all three—a round, warm, living, breathing person, her face a bit anxious as she surveyed the crowd.

"Jenny!" Meg's shout broke the spell.

Jenny's face lit up. "Meg!" she cried. She said something to the flight attendant who was walking beside her, then broke away quickly and raced past the other passengers.

Meg barely had time to appreciate the wave of relief that swept over her. Jenny was here! She hadn't overslept, the plane hadn't crashed. Then their arms were around each other, and they were laughing and shouting and jumping up and down like a couple of two-year-olds. "Oh, Jenny, you're so . . . so real!" Meg cried.

"So are you," said Jenny. "And you're bigger, too. You've grown! Don't you think so, Mrs. Kelly?" she said, spinning Meg around so they were standing back to back.

"I believe you're right," she said, laughing. "Brittany, you'd better get a picture of these two before they start jumping up and down again."

Brittany stepped forward a bit shyly, her camera

in her hand. Amy pushed in beside her, holding up her sign.

"Oh my gosh," Meg said. "I'm so excited I almost forgot! Jenny this is—"

"You don't have to tell me," Jenny interrupted. "Brittany Logan and Amy Chan. You look just like you do in your pictures."

"So do you," said Amy. "Only better! Here, hold the sign. Brittany can take a picture of the two of you, and then we'll get Meg's mother to take a picture of all five—I mean, all four of us."

Jenny frowned. "So Cricket didn't come?" she whispered as Meg put her arm around her shoulder to pose for the camera.

"No," Meg admitted, hating to spoil the moment. "I kept hoping she'd call, but—"

"Well, don't worry." Jenny rested her cheek against Meg's as the flash on Brittany's camera went off. "I've got the tape right here," she said, patting her backpack. "And just wait until you see all the other stuff I brought. I wasn't sure what the weather would be like, so I packed warm things and cool things. And then, of course, I had to bring all the clothes I got for Christmas to show you. We actually had to sit on my suitcase to get it closed. I hope it didn't burst open in the baggage compartment."

"Oh, that happened to me once," said Brittany, as they posed for Mrs. Kelly and then headed for the baggage area. "It was so embarrassing. My underwear was all over the conveyor belt!"

Luckily, the same thing hadn't happened to Jenny. Her suitcase was intact, and Amy pulled it off the baggage carousel on the second try. Then it was back to the parking lot, into the car, through the city, and across the Golden Gate Bridge.

"Oh no!" Jenny exclaimed, leaning out the car window. "The bridge is red! I thought it would be gold."

"So did I," said Meg. "I was so disappointed when I first saw it. But it's a really nice shade of red. Maybe we'll paint our house that color, with white trim and navy blue for the front door."

"I can't wait to see it," said Jenny. "Have you been working on it all week?"

"Have we ever," Amy groaned. "I've got the blisters to show for it." She held out her hand to display the places where the skin had been rubbed off by all the sweeping and raking they'd done.

"But don't worry, Jenny," Brittany teased, as they turned off the freeway and into Redwood Grove. "There's still plenty of work for you to do."

Listening to them talk, anyone would have thought they'd known each other all their lives. It was the same with Meg's grandparents. Though they hadn't met Jenny before, they welcomed her with open arms, while Kevin—who knew her well and was hoping she'd be willing to play Candy Land with him—danced around, chattering about the fire engine he'd gotten for Christmas and about how they were all going to their new house to paste paper on the walls.

"Kevin's right," Mrs. Kelly said. "I hope you don't mind, Jenny, but if we're going to get Meg's room wallpapered before our furniture is delivered, we have to start work on it this afternoon. Why don't you go and change? I'll call your mother to let her know you've arrived safely, and then we can drive right over."

"Great!" said Jenny, as Amy—aided by Brittany—grabbed her suitcase and started up the stairs. "I brought some grubby clothes that are just right for work."

Meg picked up Jenny's backpack, which she'd dropped by the front door when Kevin nearly bowled her over. Suddenly she remembered their plan. She'd almost forgotten it in all the excitement of Jenny's arrival! "Mom," she said quickly. "Can we stop at Cricket's on the way to our house?"

Mrs. Kelly looked surprised. She knew about the situation with Cricket, but not about the girls' plan for putting it right. "Yes, of course," she said. "But I thought—"

"We have something to give her," Meg explained, hugging the backpack in her arms as she hurried up the stairs after the other girls. "Something very important!"

112

C h a p t e r

9

There were so many things in her grandparents' house that Meg wanted to show Jenny—the stained glass window in the bathroom, the secret attic that you entered through a trapdoor in the ceiling of Meg's closet, the old red scrapbook from the original Always Friends Club, and the new scrapbook that their club was keeping. But right now, none of those things was as important as what Jenny pulled out of her backpack.

She unzipped it the moment they reached Meg's room and dug around inside, pulling out a sweater, a box of chocolates for Meg's grandparents, a couple of magazines and paperback books, and finally a rectangular-shaped package wrapped in white tissue paper and tied with a red ribbon. It was the size of a videocassette box because that's exactly what it was. An envelope taped to the top read *To Cricket—From Jenny.*

"Oh no," said Amy, sounding disappointed. "It's all wrapped up. I was hoping we could see it."

"So was I," said Meg. "Though we wouldn't have had time to put it in the VCR now. Besides, it's Cricket's. It's up to her to show it to us—if she wants to. If she forgives us. I mean . . . if she forgives *me*."

"Oh, but I'm sure she will," said Brittany. "How could she possibly stay angry when she realizes that we've found her friend Jenny?"

Jenny—Meg's Jenny—agreed. "It's pretty powerful stuff. I don't see how anyone could resist it," she said. "And her Jenny's really nice. I think we'll be friends if she stays in Los Angeles, though I know she's hoping things work out between her parents. I got her to tell Cricket everything, about how she's sorry for not writing and how hard things were for her. We did the taping at my house just before she left for Alaska. I got all choked up just listening to her. Lucky I didn't drop the video camera—it's brand-new and my uncle was sort of worried about loaning it to me. The tape turned out really well, though. She wrote a letter, too. That's what's in the envelope. And she said that she'd phone Cricket from Alaska as soon as she could."

"Well, that should do it," said Amy. "What about the heart?" she asked, turning to Meg. "I think we should give it back to her just so she'll know we don't want to accept her resignation."

"I already thought of that," said Meg. "I put it in

here, along with an apology from me." She picked up an envelope from her desk. The outline of the metal heart with Cricket's name on it could be seen through the paper. "I don't know what else we can do," she said as she slipped the envelope under the red ribbon on the package. "If this doesn't work . . ." But she wasn't going to think about that!

It took Jenny only a few minutes to change into an old sweatshirt and a pair of sweatpants that she pulled from her overstuffed suitcase. The other girls planned to change at Meg's house, where they'd stored their grubby old work clothes. Then after a quick trip to the bathroom and the promise of a bubble bath later in the claw-footed tub, and a peek into the attic, which Jenny couldn't wait to see, the girls headed back downstairs and out to the car.

As her mother backed out of the driveway and turned in the direction of Cricket's house, Meg clutched the package for Cricket to her chest, as if holding it close to her heart would work some sort of magic. Maybe, she thought, all the feelings that were racing around inside her would be captured and transferred to the tape.

"Do you want one of us to take it in?" Brittany asked, when Mrs. Kelly stopped the car in front of Cricket's house. "I wouldn't mind."

"No, I'll do it," said Meg, steeling herself. What would it look like if Cricket came to the door and saw her cowering in the car? Secretly, she was hoping that it wouldn't be Cricket who opened the door, but in case it was . . . "I won't try to explain," she said. "I'll just give her the package and tell her that we'll be at the new house. She can decide if she wants to come over or not."

It sounded simple, but as she stepped from the car Meg realized that she was as nervous as she'd been on her first day of school at Redwood Grove Elementary. She paused for a moment to gather her courage and then forced herself to move up the walk to Cricket's front door. The living room drapes were closed against the bright noontime sun, but as she reached for the doorbell, she thought she saw someone—someone with red hair—open them a crack. As she pressed her finger to the bell, the drapes quickly closed. When the door opened it was Mrs. Connors, not Cricket, who stood there.

"Oh, Meg," Cricket's mother said, looking concerned. "I . . . I'm so glad to see you. But I'm afraid Cricket's not . . . I mean, she can't . . ." She cast a nervous glance back into the house.

Meg could hear panting and toenails scraping against the floor. It was Buster, who usually charged out the door whenever it was opened. But now someone—Meg thought she knew who—was holding him back.

"That's okay," she said quickly, not wanting to

force a grown-up to lie. "I have something for her, that's all." She handed the package with the red ribbon to Cricket's mother. "Tell her . . ." She hesitated. She was sure that Cricket was listening and suddenly she wanted to blurt out everything. She wanted to say how sorry she was. She wanted to tell Cricket that her friend Jenny hadn't forgotten her, and that she had to come back to the club. But she didn't dare. It might spoil everything. It was better if Cricket watched the tape and read the letters first. "Just tell her that we'll be at my new house," she said finally. "All of us—Amy, Brittany, and my friend Jenny from Los Angeles. We're going to wallpaper my room. It's kind of a . . . a club project, so if Cricket wants to help . . ."

She heard Buster whimpering. He must have recognized her voice. He was probably dying to run to the door and give her one of his big doggy kisses. Thinking that maybe Cricket was dying to run to the door, too, she finished her speech quickly. "Anyway, we hope that she'll come," she said, as Buster, who didn't know anything about fights between friends, started whimpering again. Then before Mrs. Connors could say anything, or Buster could break loose, she dashed back down the walk to the car.

"Well? Did you see her?" Jenny asked.

"No, but I think she saw me," Meg replied, climbing into the backseat and slamming the door shut. Her heart was beating hard and she suddenly realized how shaky she felt. "Let's just go, Mom," she said. "I don't want to talk about it."

Mrs. Kelly cast a worried glance in the rearview mirror. "All right," she agreed, as Meg scrunched down in the seat. "I don't know what you girls are up to, but whatever it is, I hope it works out." She waved quickly to Cricket's mother—her old childhood friend—who was still standing at the door. Meg suddenly realized how hard it would be for them if their daughters remained enemies. As the car pulled away from the curb, she started imagining all the things that might go wrong. What if the Connors' VCR wasn't working? What if their TV set was broken? Or suppose Cricket was still angry after watching the tape? Suppose, after learning about their meddling, she was angrier than ever?

"Just stop thinking about it," whispered Jenny as they turned onto the crooked street where the Kellys' new house was located. "You've done all you could. It's up to her now."

Meg knew she was right. As they pulled into the driveway beside the steep-roofed house, she forced herself to stop thinking about Cricket. After all, no matter what happened, she had plenty to be thankful for. Amy and Brittany, for instance, who'd worked so hard all week helping her, and Jenny herself. She was truly happy about the new house, too. It was hard to believe that she'd ever thought she wouldn't want to live there. The kitchen, with its new coat of paint and clean windows, was sunny and cheerful, she and Kevin both had big bedrooms, her mother had room for an office, and there was space in the backyard for a badminton net, a picnic table, and maybe even a vegetable garden. Best of all, it was only a short walk from her grandparents' house. She could go there to visit whenever she wanted. And she could already see how much better it was going to be for her mother. She and Grandma laughed together all the time now.

"Come on," she said, trying to put some enthusiasm into her voice as she and Jenny, Amy, and Brittany piled out of the car. "I'll show you the yard first, then the downstairs, and then I'll take you up to my room. That's the *pièce de*—whatever you call it."

"The *pièce de résistance*," Brittany pronounced in French. "The best thing of all. You're learning Meg," she added with a grin.

The first part of the tour took longer than Meg expected, partly because Jenny was so excited and insisted on inspecting everything, and partly because halfway through it Kevin and his grandparents arrived with the sandwiches for lunch. Then Kevin had to show Jenny everything again, including which tree he was going to hang a swing from and where Grandpa was going to build him a hideout.

By the time they managed to get inside and see the living room, the kitchen, and the rest of the downstairs, nearly three quarters of an hour had passed, maybe more. Plenty of time, Meg thought, as she started up the stairs, for someone to watch a short video. Plenty of time for someone to take a small metal heart out of an envelope, press it to her own heart, and read a few short letters.

She stepped into her room, so welcoming now that the cowboy wallpaper was gone, and headed straight for the window. Through the sparkling glass panes, she could see the gate at the back of the yard, and in the distance Cricket's neat blue house. But no red-headed girl was running down the pathway that connected them. No red-headed girl was coming through the gate. Maybe it wasn't going to work then. Maybe she wouldn't—

"Meg! Oh, Meg!" Jenny's voice broke into Meg's thoughts and she tried, once again, to push Cricket out of them. "This is so wonderful!" Jenny exclaimed, coming into the room and looking around at the slanted ceilings and the dormer window with the white-cushioned window seat stretching across it. She'd been exclaiming over everything, of course, but now Meg heard a note in her voice that went way past politeness.

"You really like it?" she asked, suddenly anxious. She realized how much she wanted Jenny to like everything in Redwood Grove—her house, her friends, the bushes, trees, and flowers, even the weather.

"Well, of course she does," answered Amy. "Who wouldn't?"

Brittany laughed. "You have to speak up fast around here, Jenny," she said. "And work hard, too. Just look at all that wallpaper waiting for us." She pointed to the rolls stacked neatly in the corner. "Before we get started, though, let me take a picture. How about all of you sitting on the window seat?"

Jenny's eyes lit up and she danced across the room, lowering herself onto the cushions like a butterfly alighting on a flower. There was no mistaking the look on her face—sheer envy. "You are so lucky," she said, as Meg and Amy sat down, considerably less gracefully, beside her. "I'd give anything for a place like this, where I could sit and read, or draw pictures, or just daydream." She looked out the window as Brittany focused her camera. "I'll bet you can reach out in the summer and pick plums off that tree," she said. "Or maybe—" Suddenly she stopped. She leaned closer to the window pane. "Meg," she said. "Isn't that . . ." She pointed toward the gate.

Meg's heart almost stopped. Even before she looked down into the yard herself, she knew who Jenny had seen.

"It's her!" Amy exclaimed. Meg leaped to her feet as Amy kneeled on the cushions and waved through the glass.

Brittany lowered her camera and rushed to the

window to look out, but by then Cricket was already in the house. Meg heard the back door slam shut and then her feet pounding up the stairs. It was exactly the reverse of what she'd heard on that awful afternoon. Instead of running out of the room, Cricket burst into it, the videocassette box, minus its wrappings, in her hand.

"I don't believe it!" she exclaimed, her eyes sweeping over all of them, her wavy red hair standing out wildly around her face. "You found her! You found Jenny!"

"Not us. It was Meg's Jenny who found her," Amy said, pushing Jenny forward.

Jenny smiled. "You must be Cricket," she said, introducing herself before Meg or the others could remember their manners. Not that this was exactly a situation where manners seemed to count. "I'm sorry you couldn't come to the airport," she added.

"I . . ." Cricket's lip trembled. "Oh, I'm so sorry, Jenny," she said. "It's been such a terrible week, and I couldn't think of any way to—"

"Cricket, don't!" Meg cried, rushing across the room. The same feeling she'd had in the airport when she saw Jenny came over her again. Cricket was so real. She could hear her breathing, smell the shampoo she used to wash her hair. She wanted to throw her arms around her and never let her go. But she couldn't do that yet. Words had to come first. "You didn't do anything, Cricket," she said. "It was all my fault. I never should have—"

But Cricket stopped her. "Don't say any more, Meg," she pleaded, her hand tightening around the videocassette box. "Let's forget it. Let's pretend it never happened. I don't want to think of any of it ever again!"

Hearing those magical words seemed to make everything better. Meg threw her arms around her. After that, everything seemed to happen at once. Cricket hugged Jenny, and then Amy and Brittany. Kevin came upstairs to tell them lunch was ready and that Tim was coming, too. "Just wait until you hear about *that*, Cricket," said Brittany. And finally the story of how Jenny had made the tape was told again.

"I had something made for you, too, Jenny," said Cricket shyly when they'd all had a chance to calm down a bit. She reached into her pocket, pulled out a small package wrapped in Christmas paper, and handed it to Jenny. Meg thought she knew what it might be, and she was right. When Jenny tore off the paper, they all leaned forward to see a familiar-looking metal heart lying in the palm of her hand. The words *Always Friends* and *Jenny* were engraved on it.

"I had it made before—well, before everything," Cricket explained, glancing quickly at Meg.

"Does this mean I'm a member of the club?" said Jenny, her eyes sparkling with excitement. "Because if it does, I want to take you up on something, Cricket. Meg told me that your father had volunteered to take us to the snow. Is the offer still good?"

"Well, yes. I think so," Cricket said, her eyes lighting up now, too. "I'm sure we could go. That is . . ." She looked at Meg. "If everyone wants to."

Meg reached out and squeezed Cricket's hand. "Everyone does," she said, and she really meant it. "I can't think of anything better than *five* friends together in a cabin in the snow!"

Don't miss any of the great titles in the ALWAYS
FRIENDS CLUB series: